Two Mice and a Dragonfly

A Novel

How cats help a disconnected family

By Linda L. Graham

First published by Dog Ear Publishing
4011 Vincennes Road
Indianapolis, IN 46268
www.dogearpublishing.net

ISBN: 978-145756-813-8

Library of Congress Control Number: 2019933269

This book is a work of fiction. Places, events, and situations in this book are purely fictional and any resemblance to actual persons, living or dead, is coincidental.

This book is printed on acid-free paper.

Printed in the United States of America

Terrie Rayder
271 N. Division Ave.
Holland, MI 49424

Also by Linda L. Graham

Indiana Summer:
From Cornfields and Lightning Bugs

A Memoir

For Laura and her boys,

Love as always

In memory of Bootsie,
a nanny cat

Prologue

September 2017

"There are two means of refuge from the miseries of life: music and cats."

—Albert Schweitzer

My daughter and I watched as three men attempted to load the Baldwin piano onto a truck. "I remember how Dad would turn the piano on end to maneuver it into a moving truck," Jasmine commented, as we watched the men struggling to get the old upright positioned and loaded onto the truck. Jasmine and her family were moving, and I had given her the Baldwin ten years prior for her to enjoy and for her children to learn to play.

"Yeah, he was the strongest man I ever knew," I answered calmly. She looked at me and we both smiled sadly. I stared knowingly into her face, and saw a tear slip down her cheek. My own cheek felt moist as well.

"Dad hucked that thing around during all of our moves when I was a kid." We stood there, hearing the movers straining to get the piano into the truck. "I can't watch," she said, turning away. "I can just see it rolling back down and splintering all over the pavement."

"I'll watch—it doesn't bother me. I'll stand here so they are mindful to be careful."

I was reminded of when Sean had hauled that piano everywhere, including the three houses while living in Las Vegas for only nine months. He never complained—he just knew it had to go with us. It was rather sad to see the condition of the old Baldwin, now more of a worthless ruin, after all the moves, all the loving care of it-- I always kept it tuned and in excellent shape. The glass dragonfly had remained on top of the piano until I gave the piano to Jasmine, the figurine surviving the moves in carefully wrapped tissue paper. After I had sent the piano to Jasmine's house, her toddler broke some of the lovely ivory keys and wooden hammers inside of it with excessive pounding. The piano was at least one hundred years old, but it still stood regally, tall and elegant, a remnant of a finer era.

The men finally got the piano in the truck and unloaded it into the new house's garage. That's as far as it went; the new house wouldn't allow its entry; it just wouldn't go through the narrow hallway. The piano sat forlorn and sad in the garage, its journey at an end.

We moved too many times to count, all those many years ago, and every time, Sean loaded and placed the heavy antique gently into each new home, never once damaging it and only slightly altering its pitch. He never complained about the burdensome task. He just rented a piano dolly and moved the albatross instrument--sometimes on his own or occasionally with the help of a friend. He didn't seem to mind shuffling the piano from house to house and possessed a Herculean strength. He grinned, shrugged, and lifted. With all his impatience at many things in life, including me, why had Sean done that? I pondered the question as I stood witnessing this latest move of the old piano.

When we married, Sean made a promise to Dad. "Mr. Crane, I will take care of Tully." A few years after our wedding, my parents bought and gave me the piano, purchased from a well-to-do elderly friend of theirs. I promised the friend that I would care for the instrument. To own a piano and have one in my house symbolized happiness, music, and grace. I didn't necessarily need to play it every day, but I loved to see it, positioned in all its regal dignity in my living room, where I placed the shiny glass dragonfly on top. I dearly loved the vintage piano, which had been well-preserved and cared for all its life;

it promised both elegance and class to those who learned to play it. Both of my children took lessons and practiced on the old Victorian era instrument, but it was Jasmine who seemed to thrive on piano music, continuing to take lessons for many years. Eventually, I gave the Baldwin to Jasmine as her own. I had hoped that one day her children, too, would learn to love it and play music on it. That didn't happen, and the old, unwanted derelict sat abandoned in the garage.

As I stared at it in the cluttered garage, the answer to my question hit me: Sean loved me. That's why he had made the arduous moves with the piano--they were for me. It was his expression of love and affirmation. I had never thanked him for this selfless symbol of devotion but lost my chance; he died fourteen years ago. Watching the piano get moved this final time opened a chamber in my heart, unexplored until that moment. Grief at our broken marriage flooded over me as I cried, at long last. I saw clearly at that moment, Sean's act of commitment to me. He had never once objected to the heavy beast's awkward weight.

It was then that I understood regret--and love.

Part One

One

1978

"I am the dragonfly rising on the wings of unlocked dreams on the verge of magical things."

—Aimee Stewart

I met him at the end of my junior year of high school at a dance, the last dance before the summer of June 1978. When I first saw him, he was standing across the dance floor with his friend, chatting with two girls. I recognized the girls, who attended my school, but not the guys. Obviously, they were attending as the girls' dates. He was the taller of the two boys, lean and lanky, with wavy black hair, but cute in a rakish sort of way. Later, up close, I saw his electric blue eyes. Abruptly, as if sensing my stare, Sean glanced my way and smiled. His eyes were at once arresting, but friendly, and his smile broke over his face like an embrace. I smiled back shyly, feeling embarrassed that he had caught me looking at him. Soon, the girls left for the restroom, and the taller one said something to his male friend, and zigzagged across the dance floor, dodging dancers, but aiming straight for me. "Hi, I'm Sean." I noticed his disarming grin and was overcome with curiosity about this young man.

"Hi." I giggled a little, uncertain about the way he had ditched his friend and his date.

"So, what's your name?" he persisted, standing a little too close to my chair for comfort. I stood up to meet his gaze a little better, although after standing, I realized that he was at least a head and a half taller than I, at a mere five-foot one. *He must be at least six-two*, I realized then.

"Tully," I answered, embarrassed, since people at school made fun of my name, calling me "Silly Tully." The name was short for my given name, Tullia, which I had detested from the moment I entered kindergarten. I adopted the name Tully, which didn't really help much, but it stuck.

"Tully?" he repeated, chuckling a little. "Cute name. So," he went on, "I came here to the dance to meet the friend of Tim's girlfriend, Angela," he said, nodding his head back toward the other guy. But she and I aren't hitting it off—you know what I mean?" He studied my face for an answer.

"Uh, right, sure."

"Want to dance?"

"Okay, I guess." I felt awkward--I didn't know him and here he was someone else's date. As we danced, he spoke softly into my ear, but I couldn't hear very well due to the loud music. He was droning on about himself, smiling and guiding me through the music, a slow one, for which I was grateful. The song ended abruptly, and we walked back to my seat.

"My friend Tim," he glanced again across the room to Tim, who was staring at us, "has a car. Would you like to join us for lunch this Saturday, and go to Burger Town?" Sean fixed his iridescent eyes on mine, and it was impossible to resist.

"Probably. But first, how old are you and are you still in high school?" I was seventeen and graduating next year.

"Fair question. Uh, I'm nineteen and graduated a year ago last June. But shh'" he put his finger to his lips. "Don't tell anybody. I'm not supposed to be here since I already graduated. At least, that's what Angela told me. She snuck me in through the back door."

"Oh, okay. I know Mom will ask your age. I'll check with her and let you know. Call me Friday." We exchanged phone numbers by writing them down on the palms of our hands with a borrowed pen, and he sauntered back across the dance floor. We danced two more times that evening, and I was positive Mom would agree to let me go. She had to. I liked Sean.

***

Once home, I asked Mom if I could go out with Sean. "Please, Mom. He seems really nice. I like him already."

"So, what do you know about him? Didn't you say that he is already out of high school? That's a little risky until you know more., don't you think?" Mom gave me a questioning look, continuing to fold clothes in the laundry room.

"Well, true. But a couple of girls in my class know him and his friend. I'm sure he's a nice person." I was begging at this point, but I really had a good feeling about Sean.

"All right, since it will be a daytime date. But your dad and I need to meet him before you head out." With that, she finished the folding, and walked back into the kitchen.

"Thanks, Mom. You're the greatest!" I gave her a quick hug and skipped to my room. I hoped he would call, so we could set up the date. I supposed that Mom knew that I needed friends in this often-bewildering city. We had moved from Eastern Washington, where I had attended a small high school. Dad had agreed to join a larger lawyer firm here in Springville and had practiced law in his own modest office in Macy, Washington before we moved last year.

When Sean called Friday evening, I said, "Sure. Mom said yes. What time Saturday?"

"I'll be there at one. Okay?" His voice was confident and masculine over the phone. I liked him already.

Saturday arrived after much anticipation. I didn't sleep much. *What was he really like? Is he attracted to me?* I ate breakfast and took a shower, spending extra time to style my auburn hair, which reached my shoulders. I tried to get my hair to flip but it hung in soft waves. *That will have to do,* I decided. I applied makeup carefully, using a soft violet eyeshadow to emphasize my turquoise eyes, and slid into my best jeans and a green sweater, my favorite. The doorbell rang five minutes before one o'clock, and I yelled out, "I'll get it." As I pulled the door open, there he was, standing tall, also in jeans but wearing a black leather jacket, looking as handsome as I remembered . "Hi. I'm ready." *Why do I feel so nervous?*

"May I come in?" His lips curled into a mischievous smile.

"Uh, yes, of course." I stood back and allowed him to pass. Both my parents were home, and Dad appeared in the entryway.

"So, Tully, will you introduce us?" Dad said, arms folded, a fake serious look on his face. Mom came around the corner from the kitchen, drying her hands on a towel. She looked at me expectantly, awaiting the introduction.

"Uh, so this is Sean McMillen. Sean, these are my parents, Ray and Vicki Crane." It all sounded so formal, but I decided to use the full names.

"Nice to meet you, Mr. and Mrs. Crane." Sean replied, shaking hands with both. "I'll have her back whenever you say. Don't worry about her."

"That's good," my dad said. "Just be back in time for dinner at six." I flashed Dad a grin, and we disappeared out the door before there were any further instructions. Tim and his date were waiting in the car. At least, my parents didn't insist on meeting them, too. Sean and I jumped into the back seat, and Tim drove off with a lurch. I hung on to the door handle to keep from falling onto Sean's lap as Tim careened around the corner. I already knew Tim's date slightly, since Sharon and I were in the same English class. We talked about the upcoming class assignment until arriving at Burger Town, and then sat at a table to eat. I was tense and picked at my food. I could tell that Sharon resented the fact that her best friend, Angela, was dumped by

Sean for me. Finally, everyone was finished, and Sean suggested we take a walk in the nearby city park--he seemed to read my mind to get away from Sharon and Tim. Sean and I headed out to the park, while Sharon and Tim eventually followed a few minutes later. The park was across the street and down a hill. As with most city parks, it boasted paved walkways lined with shade trees. Grassy areas lined the trails. Towards the back side of the greenways we discovered a duck pond. Sun rays bounced off the water, reflecting at us. Sean and I meandered our way to the pond, and it was here that he took hold of my hand.

"It's great to be with you, Tully," he said, smiling down at me. My first instinct was to pull my hand away. He was moving a bit fast for me, yet, I rather liked the feeling—so I submitted and put my hand into his.

I decided to agree with him, saying, "I like being here with you, too." We found a bench overlooking the pond and sat down. Silently we watched as ducks swam, occasionally sticking their heads beneath the water to look for food, bottoms up. A mother duck propelled near us with her six little ducklings paddling close behind. We chuckled and pointed to the baby ducks, watching for a while as they frolicked in the water. "I enjoy watching how dependent the babies are on the mother. And she seems to love caring for her babies—so rewarding. Don't you agree?" I turned to look directly at him for a moment to see if he understood me.

His facial expression was unreadable. "Uh, sure, Tully. I just like being with you here overlooking the pond. Cool." I raised my eyebrows at his cluelessness, but he didn't seem to notice. He didn't get what I meant, but I didn't want to spoil the moment. We had plenty of time later to speak of the future—if there was a future for the two of us. I dropped the topic and contented myself with sitting there with him. He put his arm around me as we continued to watch the ducks. It was as if time stood still sitting on the bench--no one else mattered to either of us. We just enjoyed the moment. I had no idea what had happened to Tim and Sharon and didn't care. I was here with Sean, and it seemed that we should always be together—I knew it even from this first magical day in the park.

"Look, Tully." Sean pointed to a single dragonfly, flitting over the water, lighting here and there, its iridescent wings catching in the sunlight, a myriad of brilliant purples, greens, and blues. "Do you see it?"

"Yes-- it's beautiful!"

"I think it's a sign for us. Don't you?" Sean squeezed my hand, waiting for me to answer. "I don't see a dragonfly very often, and when I do, it seems to be for a special reason."

My eyes widened, and I glanced down at my hands before answering. I looked up into his face to see if he was serious—he seemed earnest. "Yes, a sign for us. I like that." Before I could finish my sentence, Sean leaned in closer, kissing me. I surprised myself by returning it, his lips tasting like drops of new rain. The touch of his lips made me thirsty for more, arousing a sensation I had never felt before. When he broke off the kiss, we continued to stare at the solitary dragonfly. Then it flitted away to the center of the pond, where we couldn't see it anymore. We stayed awhile longer, just sitting on the wooden seat, enjoying the sunshine, the idyllic pond, complete with lily pads, trees overhead, and birds singing. His arm wound around my shoulders tighter.

"I will remember this day always," Sean declared.

"Me too."

The spell broke when out of nowhere Tim and Sharon appeared. "There you two are! We've been looking for you." Startled, I scooted a little away from Sean, embarrassed to think that Tim and Sharon may have seen us kissing. Tim sauntered up, holding Sharon's hand. "We took a hike over there down that trail." He pointed in the direction, a little breathless from the exertion. Sharon nodded in affirmation. "Why don't we go back over across the street and do a little shopping? We have time." Relieved to avoid a possible discussion on what we had been up to, Sean and I agreed, and we all made our way back to the downtown area, where there were several small shops and businesses. Sean and I suggested meeting up with Tim and Sharon in an hour, so we split up.

We walked lazily along, window shopping, until we came to a gift shop with glass figurines in the window case. "Let's go in here," Sean suggested. It was there we both saw it on a small shelf--a glass figurine of a dazzling dragonfly, reflecting the colors we had just observed on the pond: radiant purples, greens, and blues, and about three inches tall. "This is it! Our sign, together, forever," he said simply. The clerk wrapped it carefully, placed it in a bag, and handed it to me.

"Thank you, Sean. I love it!" I gazed into his eyes, and he smiled back, clearly contented.

"You are so welcome. I know we are meant for one another." I wanted to believe him, so I did. Later, at home, I opened the bag with the carefully wrapped little dragonfly, placing it on my dresser. A rainbow of color caught light from my lamp and winked back at me--the promise of our future.

Two

1979

Sean and I fell crazy in love as only teenagers can. We saw each other as much as my parents allowed, which was two times a week. During the other days, we talked by phone. Since Sean lived on the opposite side of town, he needed transportation. His friend, Tim, wasn't always available with his car, so Sean began saving for a car by working two jobs. That limited our visits. Several months later, during one of our phone conversations, Sean announced, "Tully, I bought a car--I'll drive it over to show you Friday. You're going to love it!"

"I'm sure that I will," I assured him. "I can hardly wait!" A car. We could go more places than when double dating with Tim and Sharon. On Friday, I heard the car approaching from a distance, hearing its oversized engine and dual chrome exhaust system. When Sean pulled up to my house, the vehicle shook from the huge engine, which purred loudly even in neutral. As he shut it down, I saw his wide, proud grin. When he jumped out, I took in the gleaming, pearl-white custom paint. The car was a '68 Mustang—the envy of young males.

"I plan to redo the interior with tucked-and-rolled black vinyl," he explained. But that was only the beginning of his customizing. When he wasn't working at one of his two jobs, he was under his car, rigging the engine to go faster. I saw him only once a week now, as his "spare" time was devoted to the car. On Saturdays, he drove it in the local stock car races. Still, Sean saved Friday nights for me, and we went to the movies or out to the local hangout, Burger Town, and ordered burgers and fries. Sean circled around the fast food drive-in a few times first. Each time he circled, he revved up the engine loudly while the other guys looked on with envy.

Our romance spiraled quickly; we both knew that we were madly in love. One day during my senior year, as we sat in his car at Burger Town, he pulled something out from under the seat. "Here. Open this, Tully," Sean instructed. I looked at the small package, holding it a few seconds.

"What is it?" I asked, trying to imagine a nice necklace or pin, even though he had already given me his class pin. I took off the pretty gold wrapping paper, revealing a blue velvet jewelry box-- I lifted the lid and there they were. "Oh my!" I gasped. Inside was the most gorgeous wedding band and engagement set I had ever seen, both rings studded with diamonds, opulent and excessive. I was both shocked and flattered—this wasn't anything I had thought about yet.

"The jeweler and I chose each diamond to put in the settings," he explained.

"But how? How did you afford such a set?" I studied the rings carefully, realizing how expensive they must be. The rings glistened from the velvet box, tempting the woman in me to want to wear such beautiful diamonds.

"Well, I have been working a third job to pay for them, and made installments until I paid them off," he said, pleased by my reaction to the sparkling jewels. I sat there, stunned at the glittery diamonds sparkling at me, promising love and happiness.

"Oh, Sean! I don't know what to say!" I thought about my parents, who were planning on my future higher education. My grades were excellent, and I had several scholarship options. All the schools were many miles from here. *How could I go away to a university if we were engaged?* I wondered, now torn between two choices.

"Don't say anything. Just wear the engagement ring and we'll get married soon," Sean said, beaming his winsome smile that made me fall in love with him in the first place.

"Don't you want to ask my parents or something?" I said a little desperately, biding for time, trying to process this step.

"No, that's old-fashioned. Your parents love me too, don't they?"

"Well, sure, but this is different," I persisted. "Who gets engaged these days while still in high school? Isn't that a bit old fashioned? Maybe that happened in our parents' generation, but now?"

"Look, you're already eighteen and I'm twenty. We don't need your parents' permission. Just put the ring on and we'll tell everyone that way." It sounded so romantic, so rebellious, yet exciting. Sean's lustrous eyes looked deep into mine. I couldn't say no.

Three

April 1979

I headed off to school the next day, wearing the huge rock of an engagement ring. I carefully avoided wearing the ring at home for the time being. My classmates noticed the ring right away and were duly impressed. "Wow, Tully! What a rock! So, when is the big day?" Peggy asked, taking my left hand into hers to admire the ring closer.

"We haven't set a date yet, but probably in about a year from now," I responded, suddenly realizing that Sean and I hadn't even talked about dates or time lines at all. He just insisted that I wear the engagement ring. It hadn't occurred to me until that moment that we needed to talk about a wedding date.

"Ha. Sean probably just wants to make sure all the boys here know you are 'taken'," Peggy said, giving me a knowing look. Her large brown eyes locked into mine.

"Oh. I didn't think of that," I replied, feeling a bit foolish and naïve.

"Yeah, leave it to guys to think of things like that. Come on," she said, picking up her books from her locker. Let's get to physics class before the bell rings."

For the moment though, I didn't care. I had fallen in love with a handsome maverick who bought me a gorgeous wedding ring set and loved me back. Not only that, he owned a cool car and drove me to movies and restaurants all over town. I lived in a glamorous city near the West Coast, far away from rural Washington, discovering new places every week with my boyfriend and "tour guide," Sean. On Thursday of the next week of the ring, Sean called. "Tomorrow we're going to a new Italian restaurant on the west side called Angelos. Wear something special."

"Don't I always?" I teased back.

"Well, yes, sure," he stammered, realizing I had bested him there. But just in case---"

"Okay. Don't worry. I have a nice dress." On Friday, I put on my new green dress with a boat neckline and short skirt. As I paraded in front of the mirror, I was satisfied that this was the perfect attire for whatever it was he wanted to tell me. I knew that it went well with my turquoise eyes, auburn hair, and showed enough of my legs. I even had matching green shoes. Sean arrived promptly at six, sporting a new looking dark blue shirt and sleek black dress slacks. He flashed me a grin of approval as he looked me over.

"That's what I'm talking about," he said good naturedly. My hair cooperated for once, falling in straight lines from my shoulders, with just a hint of curl. We set out, the Mustang jumping to life with a roar.

As the car rumbled noisily down the street, I attempted to speak, nearly raising my voice to a shout to be heard. "Is there a special reason for you to ask me to dress up?" Instead of answering right away, Sean grabbed my hand after shifting into third gear, pulling me closer to his side on the seat.

"Well, sure. But I'll tell you as we eat." I turned sideways to look at his eyes. His eyes—I could never say no to those.

"Okay. I can wait."

We arrived in the authentic-looking Italian place and were seated at a small window table. Each table had red checkered tablecloths with a lit candle and a small vase of carnations. "This is nice," I commented as Sean held my seat for me. We ordered a pepperoni pizza that turned out to be delectable. "Yum! So amazing!" I said, tomato sauce dribbling down my chin. I dabbed at it with a cloth napkin.

"I know! That's why I brought you here. The other is that we need to set a date," Sean said, emphasizing the word *date*. He gave me the stare--those eyes again.

"Oh, that," I answered, suddenly feeling my heart beating faster, my hands getting shaky as I put my fork down. "We haven't even told my parents yet or showed them my ring." I felt a twinge of guilt, staring down at my left ring finger. The ring sparkled and danced in the dimly candle-lit room. We sat across the table from each other without speaking for a moment, the idea of telling my parents hovering between us. Sean took my hands in his. Suddenly I was aware of the soft music playing in the background, some sort of romantic Italian song. My mind wandered, refusing to dwell on setting a *date* for a wedding. My plan of attending a university loomed before me. I was still deciding between a university in Oregon, or one instate in Washington. Now I envisioned the disappointment in my parents' faces when they found out about the ring.

"So?" Sean leaned forward, grasping my hands tighter. The candle in the middle of the table glowed brightly, reflecting in his eyes, lighting up his face and hair. He continued to look at me, waiting for an answer.

"So, okay." I took a deep breath before going on. "Maybe let's choose a date a year from now so I can at least complete a year at a university. Maybe plan a June wedding?" Desperate, I was mentally calculating that a year would give me time away from him and his mesmerizing eyes, and to back out of the wedding plans to finish my four-year education. *What was I getting into?*

"Okay, I happen to have a calendar here in my pocket," Sean said, smiling as he withdrew it from his shirt pocket. He looked pleased with himself for having thought to bring it. Choose a day next June." He thrust the small calendar across the table.

"How about this one?" I asked, pointing to a Friday, the sixteenth of June of the following year, in 1980.

"Looks good to me," Sean answered. I felt a nervous wave of nausea sweep over me as he grinned.

"All right then. It's settled." I couldn't meet his look as I said the words. Silently, we toasted with our sodas and finished off the meal with spumoni ice cream. Instead of feeling elated, I visualized my educational goals evaporating. Then I thought about how I ruined my parents' dreams for my future. *Dad will gaze at me with sad eyes, breathe deeply, and say that I was making a huge mistake by throwing away my scholarships. Mom will lash out and call me foolish, and probably refuse to attend the wedding. Both will be deeply hurt.*

Four

Sean pulled into the driveway of my house and we sat for a few minutes after he turned off the deafening engine of the Mustang. He took my hand in his and squeezed it before giving me a lingering kiss. "Tully, let's do this," he said in a throaty whisper. "Are you ready?"

I took a breath. "Yes. As much as I'll ever be," I said, pushing back the pricking dread of what would happen to my college career. Looming in my mind were Mom and Dad's disappointment--or worse—anger, at our announcement. I glanced down at my engagement ring, the diamond cuts dancing in the dome light of the car. The sparkling rays looked happy—a promise of a bright future with Sean. Sean opened the driver's door of the car and got out, assisting me out of the passenger side. As we ambled into the house, Mom saw us as she was washing up the dinner dishes. She was rinsing them and putting them into the dishwasher--a first in our house. I loved the dishwasher machine—it made my job as co-dishwasher so much easier than washing by hand. "Hi Mom." I tried so sound casual, adding, "Is Dad around?" Nervous, I sat down on the couch, and Sean followed suit.

"Oh yes, he's here. He's out in the garage, puttering around," Mom answered, continuing to load the dishwasher.

"Okay, I'll go find him," I said, jumping up to look in the garage. There he was, as usual, with a hammer in his hand, building something made of wood. Was it another birdhouse? Probably. "Dad, Sean and I need you for a minute." Dad stopped in midair, his hammer poised to strike a nail.

"What?" he asked, waiting before lowering the hammer.

"Sean and I want to talk to you. You, too, Mom," I looked over at her in the kitchen through the open door leading into the garage.

"Oh?' I saw Mom's defensive radar turn on immediately; she knew something was in the air. "What is it"?" she asked, frowning, a furrow between her eyes visible already.

"Oh, nothing much. Sean just had something to share. I, uh, should say, us, we both do."

"All right. Let me finish up the dishes."

I glanced over at Sean, hoping he would say something—anything. For once, he had nothing to add. He stood close to me in the doorway, silent. We walked back into the living room to wait for Mom and Dad, sitting down together on the couch. Nervously, I sat on the edge of the cushion, twirling the ring around my ring finger of my left hand, mesmerized by the diamond twinkling each time it circled back. Sean grabbed my right hand. "Tully, it's going to be all right. They love me, remember?"

"Remember what?" Mom called from the kitchen.

"Nothing, Mom." At that moment, Mom strolled into the living room, wiping her hands on a dish towel. I observed her as if for the first time, like an out of body experience. She was slight—petite but curved in the right places. She wore snug, black slacks with a blue shirt and a bibbed apron over everything. Her hair, dark and cropped, always looked in style. Her vibrant, intense blue eyes searched my face to read my thoughts. I quickly hid my left hand under my right, concealing the ring. It wasn't the right moment yet. I hoped my motion wasn't too obvious—Mom picked up on everything. She sat in a chair across from us, staring, as if she already discerned something amiss. She sniffed something serious in the air and knew how to play along— to toy with me.

"So, Sean, how's your mother?" Mom began with an attempt at civility.

"Oh, fine. She works all day and then, I work in the evenings, so I don't see her very much." Sean returned politely.

"Um hmm. And how's your job, Sean?" Mom made an outward attempt at polite banter, but underneath I knew she was poising for a strike, a lioness playing with her prey. "What is it you do?"

"Well, my main job is working for a construction company. It's going well. They said they might increase my hours. In that case, I'll have to quit one of my other jobs." Sean finished, looking satisfied with himself. Mom just glared back in disbelief.

"One of your other jobs? How many do you have?"

"Well, three, actually," Sean boasted.

"*Three?*" Mom's big eyes widened. She looked dumbfounded. She started to ask more, but at that moment, Dad walked in. He had carrot red hair, a bit faded with grey, stuck up into a crew cut, popular several years ago. He was medium build and height with an open, inviting countenance. He greeted Sean and sat down in his easy chair, looking at the two of us expectantly. Dad took in the situation, seeming to sense what we were about to unveil. He was quiet by nature, always remaining calm no matter what. Mom, on the other hand, appeared defiant, ready to take on a fight against whatever it was we were going to tell them. She sat on the edge of her chair, muscles tense, leaning forward towards us.

"So, what do you kids want to talk about?" Dad asked, his soft hazel eyes going from mine to Sean's. He waited patiently, leaning back in his chair, folding his hands in his lap. Mom continued to sit up straight on the hard, wooden chair, ready to pounce on anything we were about to say. Suddenly, I was speechless—the words just wouldn't come out. I stammered, glancing desperately over to Sean, hoping he would say something.

Sean looked back at me, beaming his cocky grin, confident that he would be well received. "Well, sir, we wanted to let you know that Tully and I are going to get married. We're engaged already." That was my cue to show the ring. I brought out my left hand from under the right one, revealing the huge rock. Shyly, I offered my left hand to Mom to inspect the ring. Instead of leaning forward to take my hand, Mom snapped back ramrod straight into her chair. She looked like she had been stung.

"What are you talking about? Are you two insane? You can't do this!! You're too young! You must take a scholarship and go away to study! What are you thinking, Tully?" She gasped for air before continuing. "I won't allow it! I won't!" Her luminous eyes blazed in anger, and then filled with tears. "Ray, do something! Tell them they can't do this!" Then Mom simply slumped into the chair, burying her face in her hands. Dad looked first at her, then to Sean, and finally, kept his gaze on me.

"Vicki, there isn't much we can do if they are planning to be married. We can only support their decision and hope for the best. It won't be easy for them financially, but they're young."

"Thank you, Mr. Crane," Sean said, looking over to Dad gratefully.

"Do nothing? Not true. I'm going to do something—anything to stop this nonsense!" Mom was fairly yelling now. She jumped out of the chair and began pacing around the living room, her eyes bulging, her neck and face red. She waved her arms around searching for a way to vent her emotions. I tried to sink deeper into the sofa cushions, wishing to escape this tirade. *What was I thinking, trying to hold a civil conversation about my future—our future, and with my parents?*

"Vicki, it will be okay," Dad said gently, giving Mom a pleading look with his eyes.

"How is that going to happen?" Mom continued as if Dad had said nothing to her. "There's no way you can go off to college to pursue your dreams if you get married. How would you live out of town and be married to--to--him?" Mom motioned in Sean's general direction.

Mom had clearly dominated the discussion, and when I glanced over at Sean for backup, there was none. I had to step up. "Mom," I began hesitantly, "we plan to live here in town. I'll get a job, work to pay for a school loan, and go to the community college here for the first two years. Sean will work to pay for our living expenses, as he already has plenty of jobs," I paused, a lame attempt at humor. No one laughed. I scooted around on the sofa uncomfortably, trying my best to continue. "We'll make it work," I finished.

"Yes, Mr. and Mrs. Crane, I will take care of Tully. She will get her degree," Sean said at last. "We want this, and I have three jobs at present. I will work hard to take care of her." He gave my knee a little squeeze. I met his gaze, thanking him with my eyes.

"Be sure you do, because once she is married, our support ends. That's how it goes when a person is old enough to be married," Dad admonished.

"Well, this is a sad state of affairs. You have so much more potential than to give up scholarships to good schools and then work to pay for community college," Mom said, now allowing her tears to take over. "I can't bear this!" Mom walked quickly from the room, the discussion now officially over. Dad held up his hands in defeat.

"Keep us posted. You're going to do what you want to do no matter what we say," he said again. I got up and gave him a hug. He looked so discouraged—and we were the reason.

"Thanks, Dad. We will."

I had hoped to show my parents the ring, but now, as I looked at it, the diamond seemed to wink back less brilliantly. The sparkle and excitement were gone. Mom had already left the room, so I raised my hand to show Dad. "Here's the ring Sean gave me," I said a little too brightly. I waited for Dad to take my hand and examine the ring, but he only gave it a perfunctory glance and then looked away.

"I hope you will wait a year or more," he said. "At least get one year of school behind you first."

"That's what we decided, too, Mr. Crane," Sean returned. Our plans now rang a bit hollow in my mind. I went to the door with Sean, my legs wobbling unsteadily, my breath coming in short gasps. "I'll call later," Sean said, staring down at his feet. I shut the door firmly and ran to my room, avoiding my Dad's forlorn expression. I heard Mom sniffling loudly and Dad murmuring softly to her as I closed my bedroom door.

Five

May 1979

Spring in the Northwest erupts into bloom like no other place—first with flowering plum trees lining the streets, a darker shade of pink than the blooming trees soon to follow. Two weeks later, blossoming cherry trees, dressed in their puffy, delicate pink petals like bridesmaids, herald the arrival of warmer days ahead. If that weren't enough, somewhat later, tulip trees, their pink flowers shaped as trumpets, announce that spring is well underway before the white and pink dogwoods chime in. Hovering closer to the moist earth, azaleas and rhododendrons greet the observer in a wide array of color, from brilliant red, softer lavender, pink, or white, along with the matronly camellias, noticeable around the first of May. Overhead, the giant fir trees nod their silent approval, the boughs swaying gently in the breeze, whispering that all is well in the world of nature. Birds lift their voices in agreement, enjoying the rising temperatures as they flit about, carefully selecting which tree to build a new nest.

Sean and I had made our "announcement" to my parents just before I graduated from high school. As commencement day drew near, I felt a rising impatience to be done with high school. My future had already taken a definite shape, unlike most of my classmates', who didn't know yet what they would do with their lives.

By the time I walked through the graduation line to receive my diploma, the blossoming trees had given up their petals and embraced summer's green vestments. I wanted to skip over spring's innocence and rush to our own wedding—so I began counting the days. I made a calendar, crossing off the 380 days until our wedding day. We set the date for a little more than a year into the future, to June 16, getting me through my freshman year of college studies. It was a compromise with Dad, who had requested us to wait until completion of my first year. I hoped that the compromise would help Dad to be a little more on my side when the wedding day arrived.

Six

June 1980

Mom resisted every step of the way towards preparing for the wedding. I could tell that she was thinking that Sean and I would break up, and then the wedding arrangements would be canceled. Mom refused to help in the wedding plans—so while I went to class full time, studied, and worked part time, I planned the wedding. I met with Sean when I could, which was seldom. This too, seemed part of Mom's scheme. I worked as a retail clerk and asked for as many hours as I could get. Mom said that she and Dad would pay for most of the wedding, but I wanted to earn as much as possible in case she changed her mind.

I kept the wedding costs to a minimum—a simple dress in cotton voile, popular at the time, full length, in an empire waist, floating out in the back to hint at a small train. The bridesmaid dresses were hand sewn; I ordered flower arrangements and my bridal bouquet, using summer flowers in shades of violet. We would serve no food other than cake and punch. My parents had many church and work friends, so the invitation list was long. I had hoped for a small wedding, but this was the one point Mom insisted on. "Tully, people will feel hurt if they aren't invited. We must invite them all."

"But I'm trying to keep the wedding simple and inexpensive," I argued.

"You have to go along on this point," Mom asserted. "We can make it modest but invite many guests."

Then there was the rehearsal dinner. Friends of the family hosted it in their home, furnishing all the buffet style food, with chicken alfredo and a variety of salads and desserts. Sean and I were first in the buffet line; he began helping himself generously to every dish, overloading his plate. He got another plate for dessert and heaped it up high. "Leave something for the rest of us," I hissed, giving him a disapproving glance.

"Why? There's plenty here and I'm starving. The rehearsal went on forever," Sean complained.

"Why? I'll tell you why. This meal should have been on you, not our family friends," I answered. "Everyone knows it's the groom's responsibility to provide the rehearsal dinner."

Sean glared back at me, clueless. "Get off my back, Tully," he said under his breath, scooping up one more brownie to crowd onto his full dessert plate. He sauntered over to an empty chair wedged between two older cousins of mine, Freda and Joyce, who had arrived a day early from California to attend the wedding. He stared spitefully at me, ticked-off and belligerent. He set his dessert plate down beside his chair, and balancing his other plate on his lap, began attacking his food, stabbing at it with his fork. The only other vacant chair was situated next to my parents; I slumped down, picking at my food, also balanced on my lap. There were no tables other than the long ones set up to hold the buffet.

Aunt Ruby, Dad's older sister from Idaho, was seated across from me. She glanced over at Sean, perplexed at seeing him seated in the middle of Freda and Joyce, and then directed her gaze at my sullen face. "Tully, could I see you a minute?" She asked. "Let's go downstairs." I set my plate down and followed her without a word. We wound down the stairs, entering the dark, quiet basement family room. She fumbled at the wall for a light switch and turned it on. Her fading reddish hair glowed as she stood in front of the lightbulb of the basement. I saw her clearly now—her lined face and intense eyes searching mine. "Okay, Tully, what's wrong?" She lovingly continued to look at me for clues.

"Oh, Aunt Ruby! It's no use! I need to call off the wedding. Sean's a total jerk—and a freeloader besides. I've known all along that the idea of getting married at our age was a mistake. My parents wanted me to graduate from college first, and I gave up scholarships to marry this--this selfish guy." I broke into tears, clutching onto Aunt Ruby's shoulders, hanging onto her for support.

"Now Tully. That's being overly dramatic. Everyone gets nervous jitters the day before the wedding. You are going to pull yourself together and go back upstairs with a smile. It's going to be fine. You have a beautiful wedding planned. Sean is a nice enough young man, but his family isn't like ours. He hasn't had the opportunities that you've had. It's wonderful that your friends, the Smiths, have put on this dinner. They did it as a wedding gift for you and Sean, I'm sure." Aunt Ruby hugged me, and then pulled me back to look me squarely in the eye. "You're going to be okay."

Aunt Ruby was right about Sean's family. Sean's father, Barry, a merchant marine, died when Sean was five. While alive, Barry worked on board the ship approximately nine months of each year, visiting his family when the ship was in port for a week or so, and heading out once more. He died in an accident at sea, leaving a small pension for his wife, June. June had to go to work to support Sean, and found a job as a cocktail waitress which, by Sean's account, encouraged her alcoholism. June doused her conversations with salty language, and with a certainty, would be indifferent to wedding etiquette. She must have had a hard life, I concluded--frankly, I was a little afraid of her. No way would she ever pay for a rehearsal dinner, even if she could afford to--and Sean and I never asked.

I sniffled, and Aunt Ruby produced a tissue from her pocket, handing it to me. I blew my nose, dabbed at my eyes, and hoped that my mascara wasn't smeared. "Okay Aunt Ruby. You're the best! Thanks for being here for me." I forced a smile.

"That's my good niece. I wouldn't have missed your wedding for the world. Now let's go back before the others notice that you aren't there." We took the stairs back up slowly, holding hands, taking one step at a time. I survived the rest of the dinner without speaking to anyone, wondering if Sean felt the same way about backing out of the wedding. He had been acting distant in the past month, coming up with excuses not to be with me. Still sitting between my cousins, he refused to look at me, pretending to be thoroughly enchanted, as Freda told him all about her librarian job for Orange County. I heard Joyce, the other cousin, explain her job as clerk at the local Macy's store. Freda and Joyce were sisters, neither married, and lived together in Southern California. They were smiling, pleased that the groom was so eager to hear about their mundane lives.

After everyone left except the two of us, we just stared at each other in awkward silence. Finally, Sean broke the quiet, saying, "Well, I guess tomorrow is the big day. It's already nine o'clock--I'll drive you home now."

Relieved that he didn't speak about our disagreement, I just put on my jacket, trying to avoid conversation, afraid of what comments might pop out of my mouth. "I'll go thank the Smiths," I said, slipping away into the kitchen where cleanup was well underway. We rode to my home in complete silence, save for the loud rumbling of his car, each of us in deep thought over what the impending wedding day really meant. Up until that moment, the day had seemed so far into the future, and I always told myself I could back out of the wedding. It had seemed like a fairy tale idea every time I gazed into the sparkling ring on my finger. I imagined the two of us, snuggling on a sofa together, a cat curled up on either side. Now, as I sat on my side of the car bench seat, close to the passenger door, the cold reality began settling in. *We were creating a life together, "til death do us part." What did the future hold? Would he always be working for a construction company? What if that type of work disappeared? Would he have to work three jobs to make ends meet? Would I be able to finish my degree and get a good job? Would we be happy? Nothing had been discussed, really. All we had agreed on was a wedding date, getting one or more cats after we married, and me finishing my Bachelor's Degree. Even that sounded difficult, with rising tuition costs. Hopefully, I will qualify for tuition loans and repay them with a* full- *time job afterward.* My thoughts were interrupted as we pulled up into my parents' driveway. *My parents'--not my home.*

Soon, I would be living in the cheap, ugly, one-bedroom apartment that we rented last week. It was cramped and cold compared to this lovely home—the home I was voluntarily evicting myself from tomorrow. We didn't even have decent furniture. Sean's Mom gave us a threadbare, olive green sofa and an old bed she no longer needed; Dad donated an ancient wooden desk. We bought a used table and chairs, along with three boards and concrete blocks to build a bookstand, thus completing our "newly married" set of furniture. All of this awaited our arrival to the apartment after the wedding and a weekend honeymoon in Seattle.

Seven

Vicki

Luke has been gone for a year now. I still rack my brain over why he suddenly took off, no explanation, and no word of him since. I ask myself every day why he left. I try to talk to Ray about Luke, but he just gives me a pained look, and disappears into the office. He stares at his computer for hours after that. Somehow Luke's disappearance has caused a terrible rift in our relationship. We both grieve for our son in our own ways but can't seem to connect anymore.

I lie awake at night, worrying about Luke. Is he doing okay? Is he angry at us for something? What can I do, or what can Ray do? We wanted to contact Luke but there was no phone number or anything. So now what? Is he living in another state? Did he go to Mexico or Canada? How does he support himself? I also tried to contact his friend, Randy. I wanted to invite both to Tully's wedding. Randy avoided my calls for several weeks, never returning them. Again, I felt so hurt; why did Luke cut us off this way?

On my fourth attempt to call Randy, he picked up. "Uh, sorry Mrs. Crane, I've been working extra hours, and didn't have time to call you back." *The excuse was a bit lame, but I guessed that he was politely covering for Luke.*

I caught my breath, so glad to have Randy on the other end of the line. "Have you heard from Luke? Is he okay?"

"Yes. I did get word from him a while back." *Randy hesitated, laughing nervously.* "Uh, you see, he uh, asked me not to contact you."

"Oh. But, how is he? Where is he?" *I wanted to know as much as I could get out of Randy before he hung up; I bit back a sob. I was glad he couldn't see me on the phone.*

"Well, he asked me not to say. But, I think you deserve to know something. I know my mom would be sick with worry. He, uh—well, he enlisted--in the army. He's been deployed. Not sure where right now. I don't hear from him often."

"The *army*? You mean, the *military*? Oh my! Why didn't he tell us?"

"Not sure Mrs. Crane. You'll have to ask him. I need to run—leave for work in twenty minutes."

"Thank you, Randy. You're invited to the wedding, of course. I'll send an invitation later." *As we hung up, I bowed my head and cried, wishing so desperately that I could to talk to Luke. At night, I grieve for him-- dream of him—my sweet little boy. What happened that he doesn't want us in his life anymore? Why did he purposely put himself in harm's way by enlisting in the army?*

Eight

June 16, 1980

I dressed in a small classroom of the church with my bridesmaids, Tonya and Evelyn. They were a peculiar contrast to one another. Tonya, dark-eyed with black hair, was small and petite like me. Evelyn was a rather big-boned young woman with long blonde hair. They wore matching, purple dresses with empire waists like my dress, but instead of long sleeves, theirs had puffy sleeves. "Tully, there are tons of people out there!" Tonya reported, after scouting out the situation at my request. I wasn't allowed out of the room so that no one would see me before I walked down the aisle--especially Sean. Mom insisted.

"I want to see too!" Evelyn proclaimed, her eyes bright with anticipation. She ran out to look. Soon she returned. "Geez! More than you'd think could fit in there—practically standing room only!" It was then that I got the nervous jitters; my stomach turned over in protest. *Could I really go through with this?* I allowed my doubts to surface that our marriage would fail. *What the heck was wrong with me?* I glanced over at Tonya, my maid of honor. "Hey, I'm not sure I can go through with this," I whispered. "I feel like throwing up and running away."

"Oh, Tully! Don't think like that. There are too many people out there. You would disappoint everyone. You're going to be okay." Tonya nodded her head in affirmation, and Evelyn agreed with her. They weren't very convincing,

Just at that moment, Mom entered the room. She wore a violet two-piece suit with matching heels. Her hair was held in place with a violet pill-box hat. Are you all ready to go? Is everyone dressed and their hair in place? It's time!" She sounded cold and professional, rather than a loving mother of the bride checking on her daughter before the wedding march began. Nervously, I glanced over at Tonya and Evelyn, my eyes revealing anxiety and uncertainty. "Sure, Mom. We're ready—I think."

No questions were asked. "Good. I'll give the nod to begin the intro music," Mom said, not smiling or reassuring me. She was all business, as if she were directing a theatrical performance for an audience who had paid exorbitant prices for tickets.

Tears formed around my eyes; I just couldn't hold them back. Tonya noticed and reached out to offer a hug. "Tully, you look beautiful. Your simply stated dress reveals more of who you are so your beauty shines." She was so kind and sensitive to notice that my own mother had said nothing encouraging or complimentary. I reached for Tonya's arm, clinging to her for emotional support--a true maid of honor. Still, I had no faith in myself that I could go through with the wedding.

"You think so? Thanks, Tonya. It means a lot to me." Evelyn grabbed both of us, the three of us embracing in a tight hug.

"You'll do great, Tully," Evelyn agreed. "And you look absolutely fabulous!"

"How about my hair?" My auburn locks flowed freely except for a wisp of hair pinned up on each side of my temples.

Tonya appraised my hair, and then smiled. "Your hair looks perfect, Tully. Don't worry. It too fits how you are—pretty but not pretentious."

I breathed deeply. "Okay then. Let's do it." Mom took the cue and marched out of the room. Slowly, we three held hands, and exited together, walking down the dark hallway to the church narthex. There, Dad patiently waited to escort his daughter-bride, me. His eyes lit up when he caught sight of me.

"There's my little girl," he said. He was smiling, but his eyes looked sad. He was dressed in his best suit, a grey pin-stripe, with a white shirt and purple tie. I thought he looked handsome; something that had never occurred to me before—he was always just "Dad." I smelled his familiar cologne, Aqua Velva; suddenly I felt tears around my eyes again, remembering our times as father and daughter, like the times we spent fishing on the river. "Bye, sweet heart," Dad said, lifting my see-through veil. He kissed me square on the lips, just a brush of lip to lip, but a grown-up sort of kiss to say goodbye. "I have to give you away to Sean now."

"Oh, Daddy. Goodbye. This is so hard for me, too."

"Be strong now. This is your special day." He put on a brave smile for me. I wiped the tears from my cheeks, trying to get a grip on my emotions before we walked out. I was grateful for the cover of the veil. The organ music struck up the wedding march. Tonya and Evelyn, escorted by Sean's best man, Tim, and Tom, groomsman, the four of them began the hesitant walk down the aisle. All heads in the sanctuary were turned to watch. Dad took my arm, and as we began the tedious, slow pace, everyone stood. I felt all eyes on me—my stomach was queasy, legs wobbly. I didn't want to look at the crowd, so instead, my eyes fastened on Sean, standing at the front, waiting, a ludicrous grin pasted on his face. I shuddered inwardly at his expression—I felt a twinge of foreboding in my mind. He looked so sure of himself, awaiting his prize--me. I had to admit he looked handsome in his white tux, purple bow-tie, and sharply trimmed dark hair. I trembled, certain I was going to pass out, realizing what was about to transpire. I could understand why the father traditionally escorted the bride. Otherwise, the bride might collapse onto the floor. I had a momentary flash of that in my mind, visualizing me lying on the floor, fainted away, my dress hiked up, revealing lacy under garments, and Dad hovering over me in dismay. The wedding would then be called off, and everyone would leave, talking about the wedding that didn't culminate, a topic that would last in work break rooms for years to come.

I didn't pass out, however, and the remainder of the ceremony became a blurry haze. I remember choking on the two words, "I do," and Pastor Ferguson introducing us as husband and wife.

When the pastor said, "You may kiss the bride," Sean lingered on the kiss longer than necessary, as far as I was concerned, especially with my parents and some two hundred and fifty people looking on. Some chuckled nervously, waiting for the kiss to end. When we turned to face the congregation, and began our trek down the aisle, my face was hot. Sean wrapped his right arm around my waist at my back, grabbed my hand with his left, lifting me off the floor. My feet were airborne until we reached the narthex. Everyone noticed, laughing good naturedly at Sean's obvious eagerness to be married. Later, looking back on the day, I concluded that Sean was anxious to possess me as his wife: his property.

It occurred to me during the reception that my brother, Luke wasn't there to support me on my wedding day. It saddened me to realize that he wasn't even aware that I was getting married. Would he have approved? If only he had been there, my day would have been more complete. As it was, I felt the void keenly, even though there were many other guests in attendance.

The reception came and went in a dense fog, and soon we were off, in his car, on our way to Seattle for the weekend honeymoon. We had booked a hotel for three nights, a block away from the waterfront. I had to cajole Sean to do some touring; he just wanted to stay in the room in bed with me and have frequent sex. I realized that was expected on the honeymoon, but I wanted to see the sights. We finally left our hotel to ride the Space Needle elevator to the top and walk the waterfront, eating seafood in quaint cafes scattered along the walkways. All I could think about was that I had just made the biggest mistake of my life by getting married. Touring the sights was fun, but I was glad when it was time to go home. Everything was so expensive; I just imagined our finances being stretched to the max once we started paying rent, utilities, food, and of course, tuition. At least, I looked forward to acquiring our first cat together. I smiled and reminded Sean of our agreement to get a cat right away.

"Sure, Tully. Let's start looking for one as soon as we're settled." He reached across the seat and patted my leg. We were both lost in our own thoughts for the remainder of the trip back to Springville.

Nine

July 1980

> *"Way down deep, we're all motivated by the same urges. Cats have the courage to live by them."*
>
> — Jim Davis (cartoonist, "Garfield")

"Here he is! Free delivery!" the man said when I opened the apartment door. He stood there expectantly, a cheery smile, holding out a shoe box filled with cat litter. The free litter box was part of the deal too. There, sitting upright in the box, a wee chocolate brown kitten trimmed in white stared out at me with enormous eyes. The man waited for me to take the box with the kitten.

"Oh! "He's so small, but so cute!" I exclaimed, reaching out to grasp the shoe box.

"Yes, he is tiny, but he's weaned and ready for his new home," the man explained proudly. "My children named him Toby, but you can call him what you want," he finished quickly.

"That seems a perfect name for him. Thank you so much for delivering him to me. I promise to take good care of him." I was a bit amazed at the clever ad that offered free delivery and a litter box along with a free kitten. That suited me just fine, since I was a busy full-time college student and worked twenty hours a week at an all-night market.

Sean and I had been married only a month, but as we were both cat lovers, we wanted a kitty right away. I had been eager to get a cat since I was nine years old, but my parents wouldn't allow me to have one.

Our apartment was small, but a kitten wouldn't take up much room--or so we thought. Before long, Toby was racing around the perimeter of the living room, scaling along the walls as he ran. It was so entertaining that before long, our college friends and neighbors dropped by just to watch. Toby would stop for a moment, look over at us, trill in excitement, and take off again, whirling round and round the living room, banking off the walls as we laughed. He loved an audience. Thus, began the first of many cats during my adult life.

After a year, Sean and I moved to our first purchased home. Of course, Toby came with us. As a grown cat, he was territorial as well as very loyal to us. I realized just how territorial one day when I happened to be home during the garbage pickup. I overheard the garbage collectors yelling in the back, and I rushed out to look. There was Toby in a full arch, fur standing on end, his tail three times the normal size, hissing, fangs revealed, turning sideways and rushing at the men by jumping towards them. He was protecting my garbage cans.

"It's okay, Toby," I said, trying to calm him down so the men could do their job. But Toby wouldn't relent and let them pass. It took several more minutes before the cat grudgingly backed down, so the men could pick up the cans.

We decided to move to the other side of Springville after two years, and sold our first house, purchasing a house on a large treed lot but also on a busy road. Toby didn't understand about busy roads and was soon killed by a car in front of our house. I was heartbroken. Sean wouldn't allow me to see the dead cat, quietly burying him in our yard under a tree. He was truly a gentleman when it came to my feelings for cats; he knew how much it had meant to me to be able to have a cat in my life.

Sean and I were already having many disagreements, but the one thing we did agree on was that it was necessary to have one or more cats—we both loved them. Right away, I looked for another cat. We decided on an adult cat instead of another kitten. I located one that sounded interesting, but first we had to be interviewed in our home to see if we were suitable pet parents. That is when Penelope came to live with us. She was a year old, recently a mother of kittens, and then spayed. She understood human babies instinctively and became a little nanny after our girls came along.

Ten

1983

My brother Luke, six years older than I, had left home the year before Sean and I married. None of us had heard from him since. My parents were crushed and didn't understand why Luke had excommunicated us. I didn't get it either. Mom had finally got it out of Luke's friend, Randy, that he had joined the army and had been deployed overseas. Once every few months, Randy would get in touch to let us know that he had heard from Luke. My parents pinned all their hopes and dreams on me after that, believing that my road to success lay in higher education. My graduation in journalism was a victory for all of us: my parents, for me, since I proved to them that I could get an education while being married—and for Sean, who had made the promise that he would support me through college.

In June, the month that I received my degree, Sean insisted that we try to have a baby. I wasn't so sure that I was ready for that. After all, I had just graduated and was hoping to find my dream job in journalism. "Come on, Tully, we need to start our family sometime. Why wait until we are older? We got married three years ago. It's time, don't you think?"

It was seven o'clock in the morning. I had just awakened, my first cup of coffee in hand, as I nibbled on a piece of toast. My hair stood on end in a thick, messy, lion-like mass. Sean drank coffee for breakfast but ate no food. He was dressed for work, and looked over his mug at me, searching my face for a reaction. "It seems a little early in the day to be having such a critical discussion."

"Come on—when else do we have time to talk? I get home too late at night to hold serious conversations." He grinned good naturedly, waiting for my answer.

"Oh, all right. We can try. But it doesn't mean anything will happen."

Sean beamed at me. "That's my girl. It'll be great to have someone to teach basketball to—or baseball."

"Even if it's a girl?" I teased back.

"Sure. Doesn't matter at all." He ruffled my mass of hair and jumped up to leave for work. "Wait up for me. Let's start tonight!" he said, his eyebrows raised knowingly. He gave me a peck on the cheek and left. I sat there, pondering the thought of having a baby, but thinking that it surely wouldn't really happen—it didn't seem real.

I waited up for him that night, anticipating a romantic interlude. I got out the candles, selected music to play, showered and dressed in my sexiest nightie, a mint green see-through one that reached only to my mid thighs. I watched the late news, but still no Sean. He usually got off work from the warehouse by ten and was home by half past. At midnight, there was still no sign of him. I switched to reading a novel for another half hour, and then shut off the light, lying awake. He finally stumbled in at one o'clock, bringing in with him a smelly cloud of alcohol. He also appeared to be in a bad mood. "You still awake? You're never up this late." He threw his jacket on the floor and appeared annoyed.

"I thought we had a 'date,' I answered, stung by his gruffness.

"Well, it's late—I'm tired."

"Not too tired to stop off somewhere, I see."

"Yeah, the boys needed to talk about work," his tongue slurred the words. "Some of us may get laid off." I felt rebuffed—he barely looked at me as he prepared to settle down for the night, preferring his easy chair to the bed. He clicked on the T.V., snubbing me entirely. This wasn't the first time he had come home this way--angry, a bit drunk, and brushing me aside. This time, I wasn't taking it. I got out my suitcase and began packing. After filling one, I decided to go for another one, which was upstairs in the storage area. As I returned with it, Sean stopped me halfway down the stairs. He grabbed it out of my hand. "You're not going anywhere." His voice sounded menacing. "Go back to bed."

"I will not. I'm going to either my mother's or a hotel, and you won't stop me. I'm changing first, however," I said, realizing I was still wearing the short negligee, looking down at it and feeling like a fool for putting it on in the first place. I wanted to pursue my career, not be tied down to having a baby.

"No, you're not!" Sean roared, snatching the suitcase and pushing me. I nearly fell down the stairs, catching myself in time, grabbing the hand railing. He lumbered down the stairs and into the bedroom, retrieving the other already filled suitcase, and tore out of the back door to the yard. I ran after him, sobbing, foolishly attempting to retrieve the luggage from his hands. He took them to the trash can, and before I could stop him, threw down the suitcases and leaped on them, jumping on them in his huge work boots, smashing them flat. I saw his face, ablaze in anger. My clothes stuck out of the one I had packed, the garments instantly becoming dirty and torn.

"Oh, I hate you for this!" I screamed. "We never should have gotten married! I'm still going to Mom's." I cried uncontrollably.

"No, you're not. I thought I made that clear." We were shouting outside, but I was freezing cold in the nightie. I rushed back in, grabbing a grocery bag to put more clothes into so I could leave. Then I remembered my clothes outside. I didn't want them going to the garbage, so I dashed back out to save them. Sean grabbed my arm. "Stay! Please! Let's talk." He looked pained and spent.

My adrenaline was pumping, and I felt winded. His touch on my arm slowed me down enough to take a deep breath. "Okay, but you seem too drunk to talk properly."

"Can we talk in the morning? I'll go in late. Promise. I'm sorry." The regret and anguish were evident in his eyes.

"Okay, but it's going to be hard for me to sleep with all this hanging over us." He took my hand and led me back into the house. Soon he collapsed in the chair and was sleeping. I watched him, amazed at how fast he could fall asleep. Then again, I had never drunk that much.

The next morning, we talked over black coffee and toast. Things would be better, Sean assured me. No mention was made about a lay-off at work. I agreed to try to have a baby.

***

Six months ticked by as we waited for a pregnancy that didn't happen. I decided to begin my search for a full-time job with local newspapers, and in the meantime, kept my part-time job as a retail clerk. Nothing in the way of a full-time job turned up. After an additional six months of no pregnancy, Sean insisted that I see my doctor. Dr. Connelly examined me and ran some tests, calling back in four days with the results. "Tully, I regret to say that likely, you will never be able to conceive." When I heard this, my first reaction was sadness. Then, I felt relieved in a selfish sort of way. I no longer had to worry about having a baby and interrupting my career.

Instead of voicing my thoughts, I asked instead, "So what can we do now?"

"Well, many couples in your situation decide to adopt, rather than keep waiting and hoping indefinitely. I can recommend you to an agency that will help. However, first you must be willing to be a foster parent for as long as eighteen months, and then if the biological parents agree, you may adopt. It's sort of a trial period. But," he paused, "the biological parents can take the child back after the trial period as well."

"I don't know," I answered slowly, my thoughts racing to keep up with the news and the adoption idea. "Sounds complicated. Especially if the parents decide to take the child back. That would be hard emotionally, wouldn't it?"

"Admittedly, that is a big risk, but usually there are extenuating circumstances for why the parents gave up the child in the first place, or why the child was taken from them."

"I'll speak to Sean about it. We'll have to do some serious thinking. I'm still shocked about the medical results." I paused, feeling a bit overwhelmed, and then said, "Thank you, doctor."

"I realize this is a lot to process all at once. You two are young; take your time deciding what to do. And who knows? Miracles do happen."

After the phone call, I surprised myself that I felt disappointed. *I should be relieved,* I kept telling myself. *I can pursue my career and not worry about getting pregnant.* But there it was anyway. I regretted to tell Sean; I knew he would take it hard.

Sean arrived home around midnight, but I waited up for him, sipping on tea and reading. When he walked in, he looked exhausted, but his eyes lit up when he saw that I was awake. "Hi. What are you doing awake?"

I sighed, wondering where to begin. "Sean, I need to tell you about my lab results. Dr. Connelly's office called with some bad news, I guess you would say." I stammered, searching for the right words. "He says I won't be able to conceive." I looked up into Sean's tired face. He stared back, as if not believing.

"He said what?"

"You heard it right. No kids for me. Or us. It won't happen." I looked down at my cup.

"Oh, Tully! It's going to be all right. We can adopt—or maybe a miracle will happen," he said, despair in his voice.

"Sure. Dr. Connelly talked to me about adoption. We can check into that. But I need just a little time to think this over. Maybe you do, too."

"All I know is, that I want to start a family with you. Whatever way works out." He took both of my hands in his, holding on tightly. "Come on. Let's sit on the sofa together for a few minutes." He pulled me close, and we sat silently, contemplating the news together. It was good to sit there with him; the news of no kids bonding us as a couple. At that time, we still had Toby; he jumped up beside us, sensing the moment, purring loudly while moving to stretch out on both our laps. At least, we were pet parents.

Eleven

1985

"Like all pure creatures, cats are practical."
— William S. Burroughs

"So, is this where Penelope will sleep?" the pet adoption woman named Veronica asked, looking around my spacious living room and kitchen.

"Well, yes, she can sleep wherever she chooses in the house-- even on my bed," I assured the woman. I held my breath, hoping our home was suitable for our prospective adoptive cat. Veronica held a clipboard, checking off points on her list, finally looking up over the notes. Her eyes, peering from out of large round glasses, met mine.

"I think," she said slowly, "that your home will be a good match for Penelope. That is, if you have no problem introducing her to your new baby girl. What day would you like to receive the kitty?" She then paused, smiling ever so slightly.

I had been holding my breath, waiting for her decision. I could hardly wait to get a cat since our Toby was run over. I relaxed, breathing in, saying, "Any day--tomorrow-- or as soon as possible."

"Well, she is still recuperating from her spay surgery. Why don't we say you will get her on Friday, two days from now? Here's the vet's phone number and address where you may pick her up."

So began Penelope's long sixteen years with us. I didn't get to see her until picking her up, nor did I even see a photo of our new cat. All I knew was what Veronica described of Penelope. When I saw Penelope for the first time, I was pleasantly surprised. Where Toby was a chocolate color, Penelope was black, with tuxedo markings like he had, with four white paws, and white on her face and neck. She bounced around the vet's office, seemingly unfazed from her recent surgery. I thanked the vet and took her home to meet Sean and our soon-to-be adopted daughter, Cassie.

As a first-time mother, I was a little nervous to bring in a new cat. However, I reasoned, Toby had been totally sweet with the baby- -no worries at all. I had heard the old wives' tale of how cats suck the breath out of an infant. I hesitated, but only a moment, before allowing Penelope into the same room as one-year-old Cassie. At first, she just sniffed the crib and walked away, disinterested. Before long, I noticed her positioning herself by the crib, either on the floor beside it, but more often, in the crib itself, watching over Cassie as she slept. Penelope never tired of her job, sitting patiently until she awakened, and I came in to pick her up. Later, as Cassie learned to crawl, Penelope stayed by her side to make sure she was okay.

Penelope also picked up on when there were tensions between Sean and me. Sean worked into the night and arrived home keyed up and angry. I was home with a one-year-old, working part time by day for the newspaper. My evenings were long and lonely with a baby to care for. Sean didn't arrive home until sometimes two or three in the morning, cursing and lashing out at me, the available target. Penelope, our nanny cat, sensed danger, immediately standing guard over Cassie.

"Please stop shouting," I pleaded one night. "Don't you see you are frightening everyone?" As I glanced over at Cassie, there was Penelope hovering protectively. Sean continued his irrational rantings, and Cassie stirred restlessly. Cassie awakened, and I changed and fed her. Penelope remained on high alert, watchful of Cassie, never leaving her post near her.

As time went on with Sean working late, I grew uneasy at being left alone in the house. It had many windows; I felt like I was being watched-- but couldn't quite pinpoint why. Penelope was wary as well, always looking toward the windows, ears pricked forward. One night, I heard voices outside the bedroom window. The voices sounded like they belonged to young teens but were still unnerving at eleven at night. I looked over at Penelope--her fur stood on end, her tail fur unfurled and held straight up. She raced to sleeping Cassie's bedside, standing there protectively.

The next day, Sean confirmed the intruders, locating footprints outside our bedroom window. We moved shortly after that, back to the south side of Springville, a sleepy suburb.

Penelope repeated her watchful duty to Cassie, standing guard over the crib or sleeping beside it. As Cassie reached the toddler stage, Penelope was forever patient, even when she grabbed her fur or picked her up in awkward holds. Penelope's own experience as a mother cat seemed to give her the patience and knowledge to help with human little ones. As Cassie and later our other child grew older, the cat never tired of guarding them. She joined in their play outdoors, silently trailing behind them, watching their every move. Patiently, she endured their games when they included her in imaginary events. One day, I heard the children's laughter and shouting. I ran outside. "Look at Penelope, Mom. We're having a circus!" There was poor Penelope, leashed to Cassie's wagon like a pony. Penelope turned to look at me, her face distressed, as if to say, *"Help me,"* but still calmly tolerating the children's latest game.

"Put her back in the wagon. She's too old for that kind of play," I instructed Cassie. She placed Penelope in the wagon and pulled it. The cat's face seemed to relax a bit, turning again to look at me, seeming to thank me.

No matter what the children inflicted on Penelope, she endured stoically, trying to keep her eye on their activities. She surely was the best nanny cat I could ever wish for.

Twelve

1986

"What greater gift than the love of a cat"
— Charles Dickens (author, *Great Expectations*)

"No, Cassie, you can't have the Skittles," I said, pushing the grocery cart with her riding up front in the child seat. "Here's a fruit rollup—try that." Cassie's chubby little hand grabbed greedily onto it. I took a deep breath, hoping the rollup would keep her happy until I finished shopping. Cassie was a precocious child, bounding in energy and getting into everything. That was understandable, since she was a two-year-old toddler. It had been three years since my doctor visit, when I learned that I would not likely ever conceive. Casandra, or Cassie, as we nicknamed her, burst into our lives only a year ago, at age one. She had been hard to keep up with ever since. She had snappy, black-brown eyes with black, curly hair and dark skin, a definite contrast to both Sean and me, but strangers didn't seem to notice. Our lives had been turned upside down when she arrived, but we were learning to be parents, even though we were just her foster parents. Hopefully, in two more years' time, we could adopt her. Cassie brought us together as a couple—our petty differences melted away as we struggled in our new parenting roles.

Fortunately, I worked from home as a feature columnist of a local newspaper and wrote during Cassie's nap time. The paper carried community events and news, but I wrote feature stories about local people. I usually brought Cassie along on interviews, and everyone adored her.

When we adopted our Penelope cat, Cassie was new to our home as well. Cassie and Penelope grew accustomed to one another, often playing in the living room while I cooked dinner. I was in the kitchen one afternoon, stirring up lasagna, when I heard a loud bump, followed by a crash. Then Cassie began bawling loudly. I dashed in to find Penelope, a worried expression on her face, standing over Cassie. Cassie held a hand over her left eye and blood was oozing out from her hand. I snatched her off the floor, attempting to comfort her. There was broken glass from the table-top on the floor-- I quickly surmised that the candle on the coffee table had fallen over, causing glass breakage. "Cassie! Oh my gosh! Poor baby!" Penelope put her paw out to try to comfort Cassie, meowing sadly. I carried the toddler into the bathroom, first examining her eye, but all I saw was blood. I placed a hand towel over it to daub up the blood, and then dialed 911. Paramedics arrived within minutes and took over, loading Cassie into the ambulance. Before locking the house to go with her, I glanced over to see Penelope watching out the window. "It's going to be okay, Pens. We'll be back after they fix Cassie up, don't worry." Penelope looked at me, seeming to understand, and meowed softly.

During the ride, I tried to reassure Cassie, stroking her head, but it was hard for me not to cry. "It's okay, baby girl. It's okay," I kept saying over and over. The paramedics were gentle and kind as they worked over her, making sure the bleeding was under control.

After the paramedics took Cassie into emergency, I borrowed a phone to call Sean, who joined us in emergency within a half hour. I wondered how he had managed to get there so quickly—but didn't have time to wonder long--soon we were involved in much more pressing matters about Cassie. The doctor on duty called in an eye surgeon, since a tediously complicated eye surgery was necessary immediately. After the eye surgeon arrived and examined Cassie, he came out to talk to us in the waiting room. He took us aside for privacy, saying, "We must perform a repair to Cassie's eye. The retina appears to have been lacerated by a small shard of glass; first, we stitch that up. Later, after it heals, we will check her vision and go from there." He stood there in his scrubs, tall and impassive.

I could barely conceal my tears, but I had to ask, "So, doctor, will she see in that eye?"

Dr. Hummel looked at me kindly. "We don't know yet. But time is of the essence. I must get her to surgery right away. You may see her when she's in recovery." With that, he turned on his heel, and went back through the swinging doors to prepare for surgery. Sean and I looked at one another, despair and fear heavy in the air. "Well, it's time to call Mom and Dad and our pastor, right?" I felt so helpless—I had to do something.

"Of course. I'll call my mom too," Sean said. "We have to let the foster agency know as well." We found a phone in the waiting area and began placing calls. I dreaded the call to the agency, but surprisingly, they were very understanding and sympathetic. They sent someone to the hospital within a short time. All of us waited restlessly in the waiting room. We took turns running for coffee or snacks; no one wanted to be gone long in case the doctor returned with his report on the surgery. I felt drained of energy, my thoughts returning to the accident, wishing I had paid closer attention to Cassie.

After four long hours, the doctor emerged from the double doors of the operating area. His eyes looked tired, but his face remained blank. "The surgery went well. Cassie is in recovery. A nurse will let you know when one or two of you may go in at a time to see her."

"What is the prognosis?" Sean asked, gripping my hand tightly for support.

Dr. Hummel drew a breath before speaking, as if searching for the right words. "It's too early to tell. She will be fine, of course, but learning if she has sight in that eye will take some time." Slowly he turned and disappeared behind the double doors. Sean and I clutched one another as tears coursed down my cheeks.

"It's going to be okay, Tully," Dad said, pulling me away from Sean, hugging me. "Cassie is going to be fine."

"Yes, but Dad, you heard the doctor. They don't know about her sight and won't for a long time. How am I going to live with that? What if she never sees in that eye again?"

"Well, we have to pray, trust God, and leave it to Him. He knows what is best for us all. He will be with you, Sean, and Cassie."

"I don't know if I can do that," I said, finding a tissue to blow my nose from all the crying. "But I'll try."

After another two hours, a nurse appeared, and said that Sean and I could go see Cassie. "But don't stay long. She must rest," the nurse admonished. We followed the nurse back to the recovery area, and there was our little girl, lying in a hospital crib, a large, metal eye guard taped to her left eye. Her other eye was open, and when she saw us, let out a small whimper.

"Mama," she said, attempting to lift her little arms out to us. She could only manage to raise one arm since the other was hooked up to an I.V., and moaning, she gave up. I rushed to her, hugging her as best I could.

"Mama and Daddy are here, little one. Don't worry. You will be all better soon." I choked on tears, stepping back for Sean.

"We're right here. The doctor says you must rest, but we are here to check on you when you are awake, okay sweetie heart?" Sean maintained his composure, but I could tell it was an effort. Little Cassie drifted off, and we tiptoed back out to the waiting room to report to our parents and the agency rep.

***

A week later, Cassie was dismissed from the hospital, with strict take-home instructions. She must wear the eye guard night and day for another week-- after that, during naps and bed time for an additional week. As we gathered up our little one and her belongings to check out of the hospital, Dr. Hummel dropped by her room. "I must caution one more time about her wearing the eye guard at all times for a week," he said, stroking her hair while he spoke to us. Cassie looked apprehensively at him out of her good eye. "One more thing," he said, hesitating before going on. I glanced over at Sean, who waited anxiously for Dr. Hummel's next statement. Sean looked as nervous as I felt. "Cassie may require a series of surgeries along the way for the next several years." He paused, checking our reaction before continuing. I held my breath, hoping the next sentence revealed something positive. "Hopefully, we can restore better vision in the left eye, but it will occur gradually over time, if at all." Dr. Hummel continued stroking Cassie's head gently.

"Oh my!" I managed to gasp. I let my breath out all at once—then felt limp with the news. "Are you saying that Cassie might not ever see in her left eye again?"

"That is a real possibility. You have to realize that," he finished softly. "Plus, I don't know if that possibility will have a bearing on your decision to finalize her adoption. These surgeries will go on for several years, and of course, they are extremely expensive."

"Good grief!" Sean finally spoke up. "Possible surgeries have nothing to do with that decision. We feel like she is ours already."

"Absolutely," I chimed in.

"I understand. I just wanted to put it all out there to be certain," Dr. Hummel said. "You may check out now and I'll see her next week in my office."

***

At home two days later, Penelope sidled up to me, meowing insistently. "What is it Penelope?" She ran back to the living room, so I followed, wondering with a new dread what I might find. There sat Cassie, her eye guard in hand, trying to tape it to her stuffed bear's face. "Oh, Cassie, honey, *you* have to wear it—not the bear," I said. Inwardly I was panicked—*is her eye reinjured?*

I rushed her back to Dr. Hummel's office to be sure., and Cassie brought along her stuffed bear named Pooh. After examining her eye carefully, he commented, "Her eye is fine. But here," he put another eye guard on Pooh, taping it tenderly to the toy's eye. "Here, Cassie, take good care of your eye and Pooh's. You both must wear an eye guard, okay?" He looked fondly from Cassie to Pooh.

"Okay. Pooh all better now," Cassie answered.

Dr. Hummel drew a deep breath. His gentle hazel eyes smiled at her from behind his glasses. For the first time, I noticed his sandy colored hair brushed to one side, grey at the temples where his glasses went across the sides of his head. "Yes. Both of you will be better now. Wear the eye guard all day and bedtime for now, okay?" Then he looked over at me. "In five more days, then you can switch to having her wear it just at bedtime or naps."

"Thank you, Dr. Hummel. Pooh's eye guard should help," I chuckled.

Once we arrived home, Cassie loved carrying the bear around with his eye guard taped on. Occasionally, I replaced the tape with new sticky tape, since she enjoyed taping the eye guard to her bear repeatedly. All the while, Penelope stood watch over her human charge, never letting Cassie out of her sight except to use her litterbox or eat. Penelope slept with Cassie, always on the alert. I couldn't have had a more vigilant nanny, even though she was a feline.

Thirteen

1986

Cassie's eye healed from the accident and subsequent surgery, partly due, I decided, because of Pooh also wearing an eye guard. Doctor visits were frequent, every two weeks, with Dr. Hummel monitoring Cassie's vision. It had been six months after the surgery when Dr. Hummel looked up from his examination of Cassie's eye, and took a deep breath. He stood stiffly beside the examination table, his white jacket catching on Pooh's eye guard. He chuckled nervously, disengaging the jacket from the sticky tape on the guard before saying, "Well, so far, there is no progress in vision returning. I'm very sorry. She will need another surgery in a month to try a new retina implant."

My heart sank, but I felt resolute. "You warned us of that from the beginning. I'll let Sean know, but go ahead and schedule the surgery." I wrapped my arms around Cassie and Pooh protectively, envisioning her in another little pink hospital gown, being wheeled into surgery on a gurney.

"I think that after this upcoming surgery, if we need more operations, they will occur every six to nine months."

"So, we have to put Cassie through this that often?"

"Yes, I'm afraid so. Hopefully, things will soon improve."

I looked at Cassie, who clutched onto Pooh, the toy wearing its eye guard. "Pooh no hurt now," she said.

"That's good, Cassie. He wore his eye guard just like I asked, didn't he?"

"Yes. Go now?"

"Yes, you may go now, Cassie," Dr. Hummel said gently. "Schedule with the secretary," he continued, looking in my direction. He picked up his chart notes and left the room.

***

The second surgery went much like the first, except that Dr. Hummel wasn't repairing an accidental glass cut; instead, the surgery involved removing and attaching a new retina. Cassie recovered well and went through the eye guard regimen like a pro, of course, including Pooh wearing his eye guard. The result, after another six months of bi-monthly exams, was the same. Sadly, there was no improvement in vision. Dr. Hummel stood by his original conclusion and waited an additional six months to attempt another retina implant. By this time, Cassie was three years old, and spoke in more complete sentences. She did everything toddlers her age typically do, despite seeing out of just one eye.

Subsequent surgeries took place every six to nine months, with the same results: no change in vision. Cassie could see only out of her right eye. During the series of surgeries, her adoption was finalized, and officially, she became our little daughter when she was four years old. We had already regarded her as such, but finally, it was official. Her biological parents signed her over to us permanently. When we were notified of this, the three of us celebrated by going out for ice cream cones. Cassie brought Pooh and shared with him, the stuffed bear's furry face as well as hers covered in strawberry ice cream. As we sat in a booth at Polar Express, I noticed the simple happiness on Cassie. She was wearing the guard only at night now, so I could see both of her eyes. The left appeared cloudy, refusing to focus when she looked at me. "Is this fun, Cassie?"

"Yes. Can we do this again?" She asked.

"Sure, we can," Sean piped up, putting his arm around Cassie.

"Uh, Sean. I need to tell you something."

"Yeah? What is it?" He appeared distracted, watching customers file in to order ice cream cones. The ice cream parlor offered twenty flavors, all lined up in the freezer for patrons to choose.

"Well, the fact is, I think I may be pregnant."

That got Sean's attention. He stopped licking his rocky road cone, his tongue still sticking out of his mouth, and leaned in closer to me. I was sitting across from him and Cassie. "You what?"

"You heard me. I think I'm pregnant, but I need to see Dr. Connelly to be sure."

"I thought it was impossible for you to get pregnant—what the heck?"

"I know. Weird, huh? Just as Cassie is officially ours, too. So now we'll have two kids. Good, right?" Sean set his cone on a napkin, lost in thought. The chocolate began melting across the napkin and onto the table, but Sean didn't seem to notice.

"Sure, of course," he continued slowly. But we'll have to figure out how to make it all work financially, with Cassie's surgeries and now one more to take care of. I mean, the health insurance on her from the agency covered some, but not all the costs. Now I must put her on our plan. I don't know what they cover."

"I thought you would be excited," I protested, thinking my announcement had fallen a little flat.

"Just give me a few days to process it all," Sean said, picking up his melting cone and throwing it in the nearby trash can. He got up to leave. Somehow, the ice cream party to celebrate Cassie's adoption had ended on a sour note instead of a sweet one.

Fourteen

"The smallest feline is a masterpiece."
— Leonardo da Vinci (artist, *Mona Lisa*)

"Eww! Look what's on our doormat," I exclaimed. Sean and I looked down to find only a bird beak and its feet--along with a few feathers--as evidence of bird prey. Conrad and Baby sat nearby, washing themselves after their feast.

Sean's eyes twinkled in amusement. "I guess they enjoyed that snack," he said as we entered the house. The two cats ignored us, licking themselves clean on the porch.

Sean and I had adopted the two cats as kittens, from different litters. The first kitten, Conrad, was a rare male calico who grew to a very large size. While he was still young, we also adopted a teeny female Siamese kitten we named Baby. She was weak and sickly from the start, and nearly died on several occasions. I fed her pureed baby food purchased from the grocery, such as turkey. Despite her odds, she survived those first months, in part due to the older kitten, Conrad. The unlikely pair became an inseparable duo. Conrad took Baby under his care, guarding her nonstop and keeping her warm by snuggling up to her. No matter where she went, Conrad followed her. When Baby reached maturity, she weighed no more than two pounds; Conrad grew to eighteen pounds. He was an excellent hunter, leaving Baby's side just long enough to bring her back a trophy such as a mouse. We still had our nanny cat, Penelope, of course. She rarely ventured outside, instead preferring to keep watch over little Cassie.

Conrad was fearless, too. One night I awakened to fierce hissing and growling. I got up and turned on the porch light. He was confronting a possum; both animals had fangs barred and were hissing, getting precariously close to one another; neither was backing down. I knew the dangers of a possum bite to cats: they carried rabies and other diseases. I picked up a broom, swishing it in the direction of the possum, shouting, "Shoo! Go away!" Reluctantly, the possum glowered at Conrad one more time before slinking off into the darkness. I opened the door for Conrad to return to the safety of the house, and as I did, Baby came out from a dark corner of the porch and followed us inside.

Baby was so small for a cat; it was hard to tell when she was mature--she seemed a perpetual kitten. When she reached six or seven months, however, I found out that she was indeed an adult. One night I awakened to her meowing--a mournful, plaintive cry I had never heard her use. "What is it, Baby?" I sat up, reaching for the light.

"Meow!" She answered sharply, sounding pained. When I switched on the light, I saw her, lying in the middle of my bed, surrounded in a pool of blood. In the middle of the bloody mess, I made out the form of a teeny, tiny immature kitten--lifeless. Instantly, I realized that she had had a miscarriage.

"Oh, Baby! I didn't know you were able to have kittens--poor thing." She went outdoors freely and must have met up with a tom cat somewhere. It couldn't have been Conrad. He had been neutered before we brought Baby to live with us. I quickly cleaned up the bed and kept her close for the rest of the night. In the morning, I took her to a vet.

"She will die if she has any more kittens; she is way too small to carry them to term," the vet admonished.

"Can she be spayed now, right after a miscarriage?" I asked, fear creeping into my voice.

"Yes. That would be the best plan so that this doesn't happen again." So, my Baby had her surgery. Recovery was slow and difficult; again, I fed her the pureed baby food while she regained strength. Conrad remained by her side constantly while she mended.

When we moved again, we brought all three cats with us: Penelope, Conrad, and Baby. Our second child, Jasmine, was born shortly after the move. Sean still worked late and crazy hours and was away all day and into much of the night. I had little support from him and was left alone for long periods of time. I worked from home as feature editor, while also caring for a newborn, a toddler, and three cats. It seemed too much for me--I felt overwhelmed. I loved the cats, but my priorities, naturally, were the two children. Three cats seemed too much, I reasoned at the time, but to give up our nanny cat, Penelope, was unthinkable. That left the other two. I couldn't just choose one and leave the other--Conrad and Baby were inseparable--a duo of support for each other. I boasted to my friend, Della, about Conrad's hunting prowess, and that he took care of Baby. Della lived in the country on a farm and offered to take the two of them to hunt mice outdoors on her property. So, I gave away the sweetest pair of kitties I ever knew and forced them to defend themselves against possible wild animals and harsh weather conditions as totally outdoor cats.

Years later as I reflected on that time, I realized that to care and feed for one cat was nearly the same effort as three; it wasn't such an insurmountable problem to keep all of them. I often wondered how my teeny, weak little girl-cat got along in the outdoors. I'm sure Conrad did his best to take good care of her, but she was too small and defenseless to be thrust out onto a farm where perhaps a coyote or hawk got her. Conrad was a perfect cat--loyal and loving to all of us; both cats brought happiness to our family.

Little did I know then, that the event would turn out to be an indication of crushing family separations to come. Reminiscing, it saddened me that I gave away my two unique felines. Conrad and Baby were an inseparable pair that needed each other; they should have been inseparable from me as well.

Fifteen

A Northwest Summer

Just when it seems that the rain will never cease,

The grey clouds roll back, revealing the blinding light of the sun.

As the snake slithers from its old, winter skin,

Humans cast off their coats, long pants, and shoes,

Parading their bare legs, arms, and feet,

Clothed in shorts, tees, and flip-flops,

From closets and dresser drawers ransacked for summer wear.

Trees outfit themselves in summer garments of green,

Springing out from winter's naked branches.

Birds raise their young in the foliage the trees afford,

Singing praises each morning to announce the warmth of the sun.

Sixteen

Summer 1988

Sean left early in the morning and worked late into the night, seven days a week. Predictably, we drifted even farther apart. He seemed preoccupied with earning more money now that we had officially adopted Cassie. I continued to write feature articles for the newspaper during snatches of time when Cassie was napping. Now I was pregnant—a concept hard to believe but true. Sean didn't seem to share my happiness at expecting a child. He refused to talk very much, preferring to slip outside to do yard work—if he was home. He seemed distracted—treating both Cassie and me as if we were no longer important.

"Why are you always gone?" I asked when he shuffled in at two in the morning, spent from being absent since seven the morning before.

He sighed, slumping down in his easy chair, turning on the T.V. "What's your problem? I have to work for the three of us, and soon, the four of us."

"But Cassie and I miss you. Don't you want to be with us? She doesn't see you when you leave early and come back late." I knew I was pleading-- I hated that but couldn't help myself. Sean shrugged and gave me a cold look. He said nothing and walked into the kitchen to get a glass of water. As he walked away, the smell of alcohol lingered in the air. "Maybe you enjoy stopping off for a drink with friends instead of coming straight home after work."

"Well, maybe I do. At least there no one nags at me." I recoiled as if stung. Slowly, I followed him into the kitchen, watching as he drank the water. I was wearing a thin, cotton nightgown and shivered, feeling alone—abandoned and vulnerable-- carrying an unborn child. I prodded with more questions.

"Is that right? What's her name?" The question hung in the air. Sean looked down at his feet, saying nothing. His guilt was obvious.

He shifted from foot to foot, finally looking up to make eye contact. "Umm. It's not like that, Tully. You don't know how hard it's been working double shifts."

"So, it's Joanne, is it?" Again, my words hung heavy in the air. He didn't answer--didn't deny anything, so I assumed it to be true. He often talked about working with her at the warehouse. She worked in the front office. I went there once to bring his lunch and saw her. She was wearing a silky shirt with a plunging neckline, which revealed plenty of cleavage. Her long, fake finger nails were done in bright red, her face was heavily made up, including false eye lashes, and her bleach-blonde hair flipped at the shoulders. "Well, then, Cassie and I will just get along without you. If you don't want to be around us, we'll leave." With that, I spun on my bare heel, and beelined back into the bedroom. I threw on a tee shirt, a pair of sweatpants, and flip flops. I gathered up some clothes to pack, my eyes blinded in tears, not caring what I picked up. I stuffed them into a new overnight bag-- Sean had stomped on all my other bags in the previous showdown. He trailed silently behind me, watching my every move, but saying nothing. When I walked toward Cassie's bedroom, he lunged in front of me, blocking my entrance.

"No, you don't," he paused. "Don't leave, Tully. And you aren't taking Cassie." His voice lowered menacingly, but I heard the crack in his tone.

"I've made up my mind. Excuse me," I said, pushing my way past him to enter Cassie's room. He pushed me back with his shoulder-- I stumbled under his weight—my mind reeled. *Would he risk hurting me, even though I'm pregnant?* The horrible thought flit through my brain as

I grabbed Cassie's old diaper bag to fill with essentials and rushed to scoop up the sleeping little girl. The fear of what he could do to harm me produced a few tears, but I was resolute-- he finally stepped aside. I struggled to carry Cassie, two bags, and a purse, but I didn't want to chance coming back for a second time in case he refused to let me outside. Cassie roused sleepily; I reassured her in whispers to go back to sleep. I buckled her in the child seat as she stirred, and then I slid into the driver's seat. *Sean doesn't care about us anymore. Work and whoever he meets up with on the way home are his life now, not us.* I wiped at tears with the back of my hand to see the road before me. I had no idea where I was going, but it wouldn't be Mom's this time. He wasn't going to know where we went.

***

I drove blindly in the darkness of predawn, my vision partly obstructed from crying. I left the sleepy suburb of Springville and entered the freeway. I turned off at the first exit; a sign advertised a hotel with a 24-hour open desk. As I pulled in, I felt a bit foolish, but decided to go through with it. Unbuckling Cassie and hooking my purse onto my shoulder, I managed to carry her and push open the heavy, glass entrance door. I charged inside, my head held high, and gulped back my tears.

Cassie and I hid in the hotel room for two days before I finally called Mom. She sounded frantic with worry. "You should've called me the night you left," she admonished.

"I know, Mom, but I wanted to teach Sean a lesson and just disappear for a while. He doesn't care about us," I lamented. "I need to stay strong for Cassie. It was just easier this way."

"Sean has been calling us every couple of hours to see if we've heard from you. He's sick with worry."

"Oh really? Good. It's about time. He ignores us, works extra-long shifts, and then hangs out for hours after work. He needs to worry about us for a change."

"Tully, Tully, this is no way to be. It only makes things worse. Call him now. If you don't, I will. I have to--before he calls the cops."

That thought hadn't occurred to me. In my foolish anger, I had just stormed off with Cassie in the middle of the night and didn't think about how Sean would handle my running away. "Okay, Mom, I'll call him now."

***

It was an awkward conversation. I called Sean from the hotel, revealing where we were staying, and then checked out to return home. Neither Sean nor I discussed my disappearance afterward. Our routine resumed, with him working into the night, and me wondering if he was seeing Joanne. However, I had more urgent issues, being pregnant for one, and caring for Cassie, another. I managed to write feature articles for the paper at least twice a month. Our fractured relationship hovered like a dark cloud. Neither of us brought it up--we had family responsibilities now and couldn't risk a permanent break up.

***

Little Jasmine was born two weeks late, after a long labor. Both of us were fine, however, and I marveled in the joy of her birth. She was a beautiful baby with a pale white complexion instead of new-born pink. She calmly looked at me, smiling from her pink blanket. I kissed her little nose and sweet pink mouth. Her luminous blue eyes just stared back at me in wonder. My parents could hardly contain their happiness, visiting baby and me as soon as Sean called them from the hospital. He also called his mother, June, but she never showed up. I had hoped that she would; I wanted to share in the joy of meeting our new daughter. Surely June would want to see her newborn granddaughter—but obviously, she didn't. That was puzzling. *What was it about Sean and his mother?* They were sometimes inscrutable--cold-hearted and distant.

"Why doesn't your mother come to see Jasmine?" I asked Sean before I checked out of the hospital.

"Oh, you know. She has to work her shift at the restaurant, and then she's too tired to go anywhere."

"Too tired to see her new granddaughter? Wow. I don't get it." My feelings were a bit ruffled, but I tried not to let it bother me.

I took Jasmine home to meet Cassie, and my life took on a greater urgency with the demands as a mother of two. June didn't call or stop by until Jasmine turned three months old, and then not again until Jasmine's first birthday. She didn't offer an excuse for not seeing Jasmine that first time and stayed only about thirty minutes. I had to coax her to hold the baby. When June finally held Jasmine, she barely looked at her, then handed her back abruptly, saying, "Well, gotta run. I have to get to work by noon today." It was nine in the morning, but I didn't comment. I just nodded with a tight grin, and politely bade her goodbye. As she drove away, I still wondered at my mother-in-law's steely countenance. How had this impacted Sean? Now that we had a family of four, is this the way he would continue to treat us? Indifferent, distant, uncaring and unemotional? As each day slipped by, the hours Sean was away stretched longer into the evening, until he was gone eighteen to twenty hours of every twenty-four, rarely taking a day off. The girls and I were left to fend for ourselves—I felt like a single mom.

Sometimes, when I was alone with the girls, I would think about my long-lost brother, Luke. Did he ever miss me or my parents? What would he think if he knew about our little girls? Would he care, or feel happy to be an uncle? We never heard from him; we never knew why he refused to stay in touch. When Luke and I were growing up, we were close. He always took an interest in what I was doing at school, and we shared many moments talking together. His disappearance made me feel even more alone than I already felt. As Cassie, Jasmine, and I developed a daily routine, of course, Penelope provided company for me and stood in my absence with the girls if I had to do something like run to the bathroom or take a shower. Now she had two little ones to oversee.

At first, Cassie begged to see Sean, but as time dragged on, she cried in fear when he showed up in the early hours of morning, awakening her from sleep. Little Jasmine burst out screaming on the few occasions she saw him, as he was like a stranger to her. The girls and I didn't get out much, so they were accustomed to interacting solely with me and Penelope. Sean and I didn't communicate with one another except in passing; the tension between us elevating.

Seventeen

1989

Sean's affair with Joanne made me bitter and angry. The girls and Penelope became my whole world, aside from the feature articles I managed to crank out once a week for the newspaper. Sean now stayed away most nights, showing up in the mornings to shower and change for work. The girls and I were still in bed when he arrived at night, and he was already gone the next morning before I had started coffee. Under a thin veil of cheerfulness around the girls, I was seething inside. Sean didn't seem to care how any of us were doing. He just wasn't there either physically or emotionally.

I decided that the girls and I would pay a visit to Sean's work as a visible reminder of the family he was neglecting. I dressed the girls in their cutest outfits: Cassie wore a little nautical dress in navy and red with navy tights, and Jasmine wore a daffodil yellow dress with matching bonnet and sweater. I dressed in a satin beige jacket and slacks, and we set off. I thought that surely, dressed as cute as they were, the girls would get attention from both coworkers and Sean alike. I held baby Jasmine on one arm, and grabbing onto Cassie's hand with the other, walked proudly inside the warehouse. There she was, sitting at the front desk, wearing a black silk blouse with low neckline, talking and laughing on the phone. Joanne took one glance at me and the girls. "Uh, I'll call you back," she said abruptly, and slammed down the receiver, fluffing her hair with her hands.

Joanne and I made eye contact. I refused to look away, hoping my eyes reached her conscience. It was as if the world stopped turning momentarily until Cassie pulled at my hand. "Where's Daddy?" The moment passed, returning to normal.

"In just a moment, Cassie," I said, still staring at Joanne.

"Uh, good afternoon. How may I help you?" Joanne said at last, breaking off the eye contact. She took a deep breath, pretending to read some papers while I continued to stare at her.

Yes, I thought to myself, *you can help me by not sleeping with my husband.* "Yes, I'd like to speak with my husband," I said, emphasizing the word *husband.* "I believe you know him. His name is Sean McMillen." I also emphasized the word *know.* I continued to fix my gaze on her eyes.

Cassie sensed something. "What's wrong, Mommy? Won't she let us see Daddy?"

"Sure, she will, won't you Joanne?"

Joanne sputtered, feigning surprise that I knew her name. "Well, I'll have to call out there to see if he can come to the office. He might be in the middle of something, you know." She laughed nervously, picking up the intercom, punching a button with her long, red fingernail, and announcing, "Sean to the office. Your family is here. Sean to the office." I heard her voice echoing throughout the building.

The girls and I stood there waiting. I shuffled little Jasmine to my other hip. Joanne didn't offer to have us sit in the waiting area chairs or invite me to have a cup of coffee. I stood stiffly, waiting for Sean to appear. Minutes passed, and still no Sean. Joanne called on the intercom again and we continued to wait. Finally, I heard Sean call back on the intercom, clearly sounding annoyed. "Joanne, I'm too busy. I can't leave here."

"Come on, girls," I said, jerking open the door leading into the warehouse.

I heard Joanne behind us, shouting, "You can't go out there. No one is allowed but employees.

"We'll see about that," I yelled over my shoulder, gripping Cassie's hand and charging through the doorway. Inside the warehouse were about twenty employees, some busy stacking boxes, two were driving forklifts, and a few were doing something on ladders. I scanned the area, locating Sean standing to the side. He was discussing something with another man, gesturing with his arms. The other guy pointed to us, and Sean finally looked up in our direction. He scowled, irritated, and motioned for us to go back into the lobby area. Then, turning on his heel, he disappeared around a corner of stacked boxes. He never approached us--not even for a few seconds. A woman came up to us, saying, "You'll have to go back inside. No one is allowed out here except employees. Sorry." She looked at us, sympathetically, adding, "He should have gone into the lobby to greet you."

"No, I'm the stupid one. I should have known he wouldn't want to see us--he never does. What was I thinking?" I felt like an idiot, dressed up with two little girls, standing there in the dirty warehouse.

"Say, my name is Josie. Let me get you and the kids a little snack-- my treat." She looked at us kindly and led us to a vending machine located near the entrance to the lobby. Cassie quickly chose a bag of Skittles, and Josie put some change into the machine.

"Uh, we can share those. Thank you so much. You're so kind." I could feel the tears beginning to well up under my makeup as I tried to keep my composure.

"Think nothing of it. Guys are all the same--jerks," she pronounced, handing over the Skittles to Cassie. "Cute outfits," she noticed, looking at all three of us.

"Thanks, Josie. I'm glad someone noticed." With that, we stumbled back into the lobby area, where Joanne had resumed her phone conversation as she filed her nails. I didn't even stop—just kept my head up, striding out the front door, my eyes a watery mess by now. My frantic attempt at getting attention had failed. The girls and I were dressed up with nowhere to go but home. As I drove, I made my decision.

***

The luggage filled with Sean's clothes sat on the front porch with a note taped to them that read: "Go live with her. Goodbye." I shook from the emotional strength it took to write it and realize what it meant: Sean would be absent from our lives. It was late in the evening on the day of my visit to the warehouse. I went to bed but couldn't sleep, wondering when Sean would return home and see his clothes on the porch. Would he go into a rage or just quietly take the suitcases and leave?

Eighteen

Autumn

The skies darken earlier, day by day, bringing cooler temperatures.

The leaves rustle ominously, brushing against one another,

a mournful melody—the swan song to summer.

The wind stirs, signaling to the leaves whispering the song,

Softly beginning, then reaching a shrill crescendo,

Then subsiding, as if realizing their fate.

Despairing, the trees bow to relentless rains--tears from the heavens,

Releasing the leaves at last.

The brown and yellowed leaves tumble to the ground, crushed underfoot,

decomposing with fall rains, fodder for future spring flowers--

a cycle that renews itself each season.

For now, the days appear bleak and cold, awaiting winter frosts;

The trees slumber in nakedness, one day awakening to spring's sun.

Then they will clothe themselves in splendor once more.

Nineteen

Fall 1989

I must have drifted off at long last around three o'clock or so, awakening with a start at six. I rushed out to the porch in my bathrobe and saw that both suitcases were gone. Only the note remained, taped to the front step, indicating that Sean had been there and left. The note fluttered mournfully in the early fall breeze. It seemed ghostly quiet—empty. Sean was gone. I stood there, staring at the note waving at me, and sat down, putting my hands over my face. Tears wet my hands as I cried.

Penelope came out to the porch with me and rubbed up against my legs. She looked up at me and meowed, sensing my feeling of loneliness. "We'll be okay without him, won't we Pens?" She meowed again in reply, and we went back inside to start coffee and breakfast, what I did everyday alone, but feeling much more so that day. I snatched a tissue and blew my nose. I purposed to turn in more feature writing than I had been doing for a while, and composing myself, called in to the paper for additional assignments. I wanted to get out now—mingle and meet people.

Next, I had to find a babysitter or a daycare that I trusted. I called around, and luckily found a woman at our church who operated an in-home childcare with a drop-in option. *Perfect.*

My first two interview assignments looked mundane: the first, a prom queen from the nearby high school, where I would ask about her plans for education and community service; the second, a World

War II vet, who had been making appearances in the public schools, explaining the times in which he served in the Navy. The third assigned interview, at first glance, seemed even more ordinary. I needed to interview a local entrepreneur, a forty-something man who owned a booming restaurant business on the other side of town. I chose to start with this third assignment.

As I entered the restaurant, I wondered how I could spin the feature story to attract readership. The story would seem too predictable-- not interesting to read. I sat in a booth and ordered a cup of coffee, looking around the business, trying to get a feel for the ambiance of the place. It had a family atmosphere, with large booths and tables; pictures on the walls depicted nature scenes, and the eatery was well-lit. I picked up a menu, and found the pricing moderate, with color photos of menu items. Soon, I heard a male voice and looked up to see my assigned interviewee.

"Hi. You must be Tully. My name is Eric," he smiled, his hand outreached to mine for a handshake. I saw into his ice blue eyes, his gaze momentarily mesmerizing me into a stupor. I smiled nervously and took his hand, which felt warm but strong.

"Uh, hi. Thank you for agreeing to an interview with the newspaper. We like to highlight successful businesses in the area, and yours certainly seems to be that." I laughed nervously. *What a lame start. What's the matter with me? It's only another interview.* "What can you tell me about how you started the restaurant here?"

It was a thirty-minute interview. As we concluded, he again shook my hand, thanking me for coming. "I'd like to ask you out for coffee," Eric said as I put away my notepad into the small briefcase I always carried to interviews. He directed his eyes at mine, absently pushing back the blond hair from his face.

"Well, I just had coffee here, and thank you for that. The waitress insisted on not leaving the check."

"Of course. I didn't mean today; how about later in the week? How about Friday? We could go somewhere else besides here," he said as he gestured with his hand, again looking at me.

"Oh. You mean go out?"

He chuckled. "Yes. That's the idea. What do you think?"

My heart was racing by this point. "Okay. I suppose I can. I must arrange for a sitter or childcare—I, uh, have two girls."

"No problem. May I call you say, on Thursday, to see what you worked out?"

"Uh, sure. Okay. Here's my number," I faltered, my hands slightly shaking as I handed him my number on a napkin. *What are you doing?* I left in a rush, wondering what I had just agreed to. Me—a married woman, although living alone now and separated—I was still legally married. I decided to think on it. I could always back out with the excuse that there was no one to care for the children.

As I drove home, I kept replaying the interview in my mind, looking for clues as to why he thought to ask me out. *Did I lead him on? Did I appear desperate?* If I was honest with myself, I was desperate for someone to take an interest in me—someone who thought I was attractive and interesting, and not just a convenience. *But what the heck are you doing? You have two small children to think of.* My mind went back over it again and again. What was I going to do?

Sean's mom, June, called to talk to Sean. She obviously didn't know about the separation yet. "No, Sean isn't here," I answered, feeling awkward because of what was truly going on between us.

"When will he be there then?"

I hesitated, not knowing how to answer that. "Uh, I'm not sure," I stumbled on, not certain how much to say.

"Tully, what's going on? Did he leave you?" I wasn't sure how to answer. I barely knew this mother of Sean's, and in fact, she had only seen Jasmine twice. There was always an excuse for not visiting, and she was "too busy" for us to drop by her place. She was working, or so she claimed.

"Well, yes, we separated three months ago. I don't know where he's staying. Sorry--you could call him at work and leave a message.

"I'll just show up there. Then he'll have to talk to me. I need some help here with repairs, and he can just get over here." By this time in the conversation, her words slurred-- I could tell that she'd been drinking. She lowered her voice confidentially, saying, "Listen, Tully, men are no good. They're always up to something, or some other woman. You try to get him back, you here? You're too good for him. I don't know how you put up with him." At that, I just stared into the receiver, not knowing how to process this. I wasn't "too good." I thought about what I had been doing, possibly having my own affair too.

"That's not completely true," I returned. *I'm not good.* "Look, why don't you drop by and see the girls?" I said it in a rush, not knowing what else to say.

"I might just do that. I had a baby girl, too. But she died at three weeks. Water on the brain." I heard her voice catch; her nose sniffed.

"Oh, June, I didn't know about that. I'm so sorry." I didn't know what else to say, and just continued to hold onto the phone, watching my own two girls play on the floor together.

"Yeah. I don't tell many people about that. It's too hard to talk about," she finished, sniffing again. I heard her blowing her nose quietly. "Gotta go. I'll try to find Sean at work later, probably tomorrow. I'll tell him to call his family."

"Thanks, June." We hung up, and I finally realized why she had been so distant since Jasmine had been born. June had related the birth of Jasmine to her own loss of a baby girl. She still grieved for her infant daughter. I had been too judgmental, not understanding her deep sadness.

***

The affair lasted only a couple of months, beginning in a wild rush of erotic encounters, always at his place. I couldn't seem to help myself— it was so good to feel attractive and wanted, although if I thought about it, I knew the liaison was based on the physical-- nothing more. That too, appealed to me as daring and romantic. Throughout those torrid weeks, Sean never called or dropped by to see the girls. I had decided that he truly didn't care what happened to any of us. He just didn't love us. The loneliness was intolerable at times, and it was a relief to be with Eric.

However, the guilt became too much, so I finally broke off the affair. It was difficult to do, but Eric seemed to understand. He had been divorced for two years, but knew about such things, or so he claimed.

I decided to search for marriage counseling for Sean and me, and tell Sean about the affair, hoping he would tell me about his encounters. We needed to be honest and work things out. I thought we could do it. We had to-- for the girls.

Twenty

1989

Sean returned home after we had met for counseling two times. At the counseling sessions, he refused to discuss his liaisons with other women and blamed our problems on my fling with Eric. "I decided to forgive Tully," Sean said, "but if she does it again, I'm taking the girls away from her forever." He glared at me, self-righteous and arrogant. The counselor, Victor, looked over at me accusingly.

Not only did I feel outnumbered, but also guilty--so unclean--all I could say was, "I'm sorry. It won't happen again." I buried my face in my hands.

Victor lectured us on our rocky reunion. "You both must forgive one another and move on as a family. Sean, you need to return home, and work with Tully as a married couple and as parents." Sean smiled triumphantly, knowing that he had me where he wanted me. He would hold the children "hostage" so that I would never do anything like that again.

As we drove back to the house, Sean was angry and impatient. "All this is your fault, you know. We wouldn't be here if it weren't for your affair. I don't see the point to any more of these counseling sessions. I'm not going again."

"But Sean. What about your involvements?" I looked over at him as the tears welled up behind my eyes. He just stared straight ahead, and drove even more erratically than before, riding the bumper of the car in front of us, then weaving in and out of traffic, veering back into the right lane, perilously close in front of the car. The driver honked, but Sean put his hand out the window, middle finger extended, driving narrowly in front of the other vehicle. There were only a few feet separating the two vehicles.

"What about me? You want to know about me? I'll be the one to have complete custody of the girls, that's what about me. You just better be a good wife and mother now, or you'll never see them again."

I knew he had me-- I loved the girls more than life itself. I had to make the best of it. I would play the role of the good wife and mother. So that was the end of the marriage counseling. We patched up our marriage--but Sean would never admit his own sexual escapades.

***

Life returned to day-to-day normalcy, with Sean leaving the house before anyone else awoke, and I cared for the girls. I still took assignments from the newspaper, and often left the girls in day care, but I was careful not to be out for any extended period. It wasn't worth the interrogation I received from Sean if I was out after dinner. I sensed that he was stalking me to check up on me. I noticed his car driving by our house and sometimes on location at my reporting assignments. I once discovered Sean's car following me as I drove to work. Before he left each day, Sean made me give him addresses and phone numbers of my interview assignments. He also monitored my incoming phone calls when he was home. If the phone rang and I picked up, he sidled over, getting close to the receiver, and listened in, breathing heavily, demanding to know who was calling. It became embarrassing, but what could I do? I was the fallen woman, and he would take the kids if I transgressed again, even though he too, had been guilty of straying from our vows. More than a few times, he would say, "You know, if we ever went to divorce court, I have many witnesses to testify that you had an affair and hauled our young children around to babysitters. I will get the kids and never let you see them again." He would glower at me threateningly, just making sure I got the message. I got the message all right—and was terrified at losing my own children, whom he rarely took an interest in. I was their caregiver and loving parent.

He usually arrived home late at night, after one in the morning., and fell asleep watching T.V. Rarely did he venture into our bedroom, and rarer still to sleep with me. He found excuses to return to the sofa, and our sex life became extremely rare and strained. He didn't seem to want or enjoy it. On those rare occasions of intimacy, he asked, "Tully, was he better than I am?" Then he would roll off me in disgust, returning to the sofa with a blanket. I felt so guilty about my past fling with Eric, but at the same time, used by Sean and unloved.

The bedroom became the scene of my most painful moments. When we attempted to be intimate, it was awkward at best, but most often a humiliating and hurtful experience. Sean insisted on doing what I considered degrading sexual activities, using me in twisted versions as sort of a punishment--or a deep-seated hatred, I supposed, due to my brief affair. I felt violated—and was repulsed. I didn't know then that even in a married relationship, a woman had the right to say no. I assumed that I was obligated to please him no matter what.

At this point, we tried one last attempt at counseling by attending a marriage seminar at our church. The well-meaning but naïve speaker said that wives must "obey their husbands." I fixed my eyes straight ahead but felt Sean's eyes boring into me as we sat through the session. I accepted the idea meekly; my life-long sentence was that of the "fallen one." After all, I reasoned to myself, I deserved it, didn't I? Our sex life was never the same again—not the joyous desire we had felt for one another when we first got married. That had lasted only a few weeks into our marriage, I now realized, and then Sean seemed to be going through the motions after that brief, happy period of time. But this was a new all-time low.

To top things off, Sean said, "I want you to visit your doctor to get your tubes tied. Right away—like call this week." His lips formed a thin smile, but underneath the grimace, I detected a new malice that I had never noticed before.

"But why, Sean? We had such a difficult time conceiving Jasmine anyway. Why take away the possibility? Why are you demanding this of me?" I was stunned. *Why would he make me do such a thing? He knows I will jump through any hoops to keep my children. But why this?*

"Oh, well, when you were in the hospital after delivering her, the nurse warned me not to allow you to get pregnant again. She said it was dangerous for you." He looked away when he said this, as if he had just manufactured the reason on the spot and didn't want me to see his face.

"Really? She never warned me of anything, nor did the doctor. It seems like they would've told me as well." I felt a bit confused, shocked at this revelation now that Jasmine was a two-year-old. Why hadn't I been informed about my condition before now? Why was Sean the one telling me and not the medical profession? I still didn't get it, but just acquiesced to what he said. After all, it sounded like he was trying to look out for my health, right? "But are you sure you don't want any more children, no matter what? I was kind of hoping for a third-- maybe a boy next time. Don't you want that too?" My throat caught; I felt a little alarm go off in my head but didn't recognize its significance. Instead, tears formed behind my eyelids. *Why am I crying? Get a hold of yourself, Tully.*

"No, we need to be content with what we have, Tully. We're done with the childbearing part. I will take you to the hospital for the surgery. It will be over in a few hours, and then you can go back home to recuperate. No big deal. I checked with the doc already and he said that you can go back to normal activities in a few days. Let's get it over with as soon as possible."

"But--I'm not ready to call it quits just yet. Don't I count? Why do you want me to do this? Why don't you have a surgery if you're so set on it?" I heard the urgency in my voice, but I didn't care. If he had to be the one to go through a surgery maybe he wouldn't do it. We had tried so hard to conceive, believed it to be an impossibility, adopted Cassie, and then miraculously, Jasmine came along. Why put a permanent stop to the possibility of another miracle? Sean's eyes held a steely resolve I had never noticed before. What had happened to him? To us? I shuddered involuntarily. I felt that as if a dark cloud had descended upon me. I couldn't see clearly.

"No way, Tully. You know that I can't afford to take any time off right now. It's too busy at work. I've made up my mind, and this is a procedure I want you to do, and that's that--just do it." He turned on his heel, grabbed his coat, and departed for the day. I was left to ponder just what was taking place below the surface of his demand. I must have imagined that I detected something sinister. I decided that we would all be better off if I said nothing more and just went through with it. I thought back to the early days of our marriage, when he was fun and full of hope for our future family of children and cats. While I stood there thinking, Penelope brushed up against me as if to reassure me that all was well. She seemed to understand more than I realized and was a support and friend for me. I hoped that she would be for a long while yet.

As I drank my coffee and looked out the window, I began recalling our past. Why had Sean wanted me to have children in the first place? At the time, he seemed almost demanding in his insistence that we start a family. I was still hoping to further my journalism career; cats were enough of a family for me at that moment. *Control. That was it!* A light went on in my brain; he had used the girls to intimidate me. He wanted children to keep me under his authority. Why hadn't I seen that? I had strayed for a brief time in my affair with Eric, and Sean would never forgive me let alone forget. Now he was using our daughters as weapons to keep me under his control forever, or at least, until they were grown. As I came to the realization, I made my own resolution. I would make the best of it. I had two wonderful daughters, and that would always be more than enough. I didn't need more children. "Pens, everything will work out. It has to." I prayed then, asking God to help us love one another and bring us together as a couple once more.

Twenty-one

January 1990

"Time spent with cats is never wasted."
— Sigmund Freud

Life continued with Sean disappearing for twenty or more hours at a time, returning to catch a nap on the family room sofa. Then, he showered and left again. The girls rarely saw him since he left before they were awake. I almost never saw him unless he raided my bed for a new version of hateful sex. Sometimes he inflicted pain on me as well as humiliation. I tried to bear it as part of my punishment for my brief interlude with another man. Sean was the man I had committed to for the rest of my life.

The surgery was no big deal, and I was up and about in a week. While I recuperated, Penelope watched over the girls as well as keeping me company on the sofa, where I spent most of my daytime resting. Sean didn't do anything to help, but fortunately, I had my mother, who came in to help with housework and preparing meals.

Since Sean was away for much of the time, I was thankful to have Penelope to talk to and my girls to spend time with. I soon resumed taking on assignments with the paper. All were great diversions. I became more involved in my church and volunteered to serve on a committee that prepared meals for grieving families. It helped to think of others and their problems—mine didn't seem so bad by comparison.

The girls were growing and learning new things. Cassie still had vision only in her right eye, but she didn't let it slow her down in her zest for trying new activities. She conquered riding her tricycle, and peddled madly down our driveway, smiling happily. Jasmine learned to walk early, and ran after Cassie, chattering and squealing. I decided that I would cope with the bad marriage as best as I could and enjoyed watching the girls discover new things. Penelope sat beside me, supervising the girls as well. She purred as I gently stroked her. "We'll be fine, won't we Pens?" Penelope always reassured me that all was well.

It was, until I got the phone call from the police late one night.

Part Two

Twenty-two

1990

It was the call any wife dreads--from the police. The phone rang around eight o'clock in the evening right after I had put the children to bed. "This is Officer Jones from Springville Police Department. Your husband was injured in a warehouse fire and taken to emergency at the burn center of St. Michael's Hospital."

"Oh no!" I couldn't think straight—it seemed unreal. *Injured in a fire? Taken to the local burn center? That meant he was badly burned.* Not knowing what else to say, I responded, "Thank you, officer. I'll be there right away." My heart was in my throat; I feared the worst as I bundled up the children, still dressed in their pajamas, and drove to the hospital. I prayed the entire way. Fortunately, the girls were groggy with sleep and didn't seem to mind the ride. I braced myself for what I might find. I was frightened on the inside, but outwardly, I was determined to stay calm.

By the time we arrived at the hospital, Sean had been admitted to the burn ward. I could see him only for a few minutes as the hospital staff was still working over him. His face, hands, and arms were already wrapped in thick dressing and gauze. I learned that he had suffered third degree burns on his arms and hands; his face, thankfully, had only first to second degree burns. His hair, eyebrows, and lashes were completely singed to a crisp. Sean managed to smile weakly when he saw the three of us. "Go home and watch me on the news. I was able to get the whole crew out before the fire department arrived." With that, he was wheeled away on a gurney. I returned home, watching the news story. Sean had been cleaning around the gas furnace when it exploded and ignited the entire building. Since he was the foreman of the warehouse, he called 911, yelled at employees to evacuate, and raced upstairs to the storage area. There, he found two more employees. Then he sprinted into the restrooms, making sure everyone in the building had exited to safety, unconcerned about his own serious injuries. When the fire department and police arrived, they blocked traffic all along the front and sides of the warehouse. The building went up in flames rapidly, the entire structure gutted by fire. All the local news channels were there to report the fire, and showed Sean being loaded onto a stretcher and taken by ambulance to emergency.

Doctors proclaimed that Sean would most certainly require skin grafts for the third degree burns on his arms and hands. Our church and our family began praying for his recovery. When he was released to return home, I had to care for two young children plus a burn patient who couldn't use his hands. Sean's hands and arms were wrapped in thick gauze. He held them upright, sitting in his easy chair, arms propped up on pillows.

Penelope, our nanny cat, helped by watching over the girls, but there wasn't too much she could do when it came to feeding, dressing, and bathing everyone. I had to spoon feed Sean during the first two weeks, since his burned hands were wrapped.

After those first two weeks, we returned to the burn specialist. I accompanied Sean into the examination room. Dr. Schmidt approached, saying, "Okay, today I change the dressings and see how it looks." With that, he unwound the yards of gauze. Underneath the dressings lay burned skin on arms and hands. In one swift motion, Dr. Schmidt lifted the burned skin using tweezers. The skin came off in one long-armed piece--raw, red skin lay beneath it. Dr. Schmidt held up the huge piece of burnt tissue. Burnt skin odor wafted my way. I gagged.

"Oh my!" I gasped, holding my mouth and running from the room, practically tripping over my chair. I thought I was going to throw up before reaching the nearest restroom.

"Heh, heh," I overheard Dr. Schmidt say. "I thought that would get rid of her." Before the door closed, he added, "Now, where were we?"

Sean left the examination room wearing new bandages and dressings; this time his fingers were exposed just enough so that he could feed himself. He flashed me a big grin, his eyes alighting on me instantly. I knew something good was up, even though I still felt queasy from what I had just witnessed. "Well, the doc says no skin grafts are necessary. Can you believe it?"

"Good. A lot of people have been praying for you, that's for sure." Suddenly, I felt like I could breathe a little easier.

"Yeah, well, their prayers were more than answered," he replied.

Up until this point, the quality of our family life and marriage had been next to nothing. Before the fire, Sean had poured himself into his job, and was away from home eighty to ninety hours a week. The children barely saw him; Cassie cried every night, begging to see him, and Jasmine, only a year and a half, cried at the sight of him. They were asleep when he returned home around two o'clock in the morning, and then left before they were awake in the morning.

The fire changed all of that. As Sean recovered from his burns at home, the children got to be around him more; gradually, Jasmine lost her fear of him. "We need to do family outings," Sean announced unexpectedly. I couldn't have agreed more. We purchased a pop-up camper and shortly after drove to Idaho to camp in a few of the many rustic campgrounds. Sean still wore the bandages and dressings on his hands and arms, but his fingers were free to work the levers on the camper to pop it up and down. In a few more weeks, the bandages were removed.

He returned to work, where his warehouse hired him to help to oversee the reconstruction of a building to replace the burned structure. Sean determined to ask for more time off, claiming that we needed more quality family time. Some of the campouts were on weekends, but others were for a week or more. It was the beginning of family vacations in the camper, which helped to keep us together despite the long, tedious hours he worked and our seemingly unresolved marriage issues.

Twenty-three

"The dragonfly brings dreams to reality and is the messenger of wisdom and enlightenment."

(Author unknown)

It was our very first night camping with the girls and Penelope, and of course, our first time in the pop-up camper. We drove most of the day to reach a campground near Spokane, on the way to Idaho, our destination for our first camping vacation. We popped up the camper, which had canvas sides and a fiberglass top. The two sides of the trailer folded out to create room for foam mattresses. We placed our sleeping bags on these. The girls had one side and we had the other. Since Jasmine was the smaller child, she was placed on the outside edge of the foam mattress, where the headroom sloped down narrowly. Pens settled down at the feet of the girls.

The campground quieted down at the first sign of darkness. We were all tired from the long travel day, so we all got into our sleeping bags and fell asleep quickly. After about an hour, I was startled into full alertness at the sound of someone banging on our camper door. *Who or what is that?* I wondered momentarily. "Mommy, Mommy," came a muffled voice from the darkness outside. At first, I thought I was dreaming. The knocking persisted. "Mommy!" I heard once more. This time, I also heard Penelope meowing softly from the outside. Groping in the blackness, I slid out of my sleeping bag. Everyone else continued to sleep soundly. I couldn't find a flashlight, but when I opened the small camper door, I saw the two glowing eyes of Penelope, and a tiny, little person outside, dressed in a bright pink fleece sleeper, the moon reflecting on the pink. Penelope stood guard next to the little person in pink.

"Jasmine, what are you doing out here?" I exclaimed, scooping her up immediately in my arms. I couldn't imagine how or why she was out there in the dark all by herself. At least, Penelope had been there with her. The cat leapt back into the camper and I shut the door.

"Mommy, I fall out," Jasmine explained in her toddler vocabulary. I was astonished; she hadn't so much as whimpered from rolling out onto a bed of pine needles. For the rest of the night, she slept close to me. Penelope curled up protectively beside Jasmine. In the morning, we examined the canvas sides of the camper. It appeared that the flaps easily gave way to pressure. For the remainder of that camping trip, we had Cassie sleep on the edge.

When we got back home, Sean purchased strong grommets with sturdy straps and installed them all along the edges of the canvas. From our next camping trip on, no one fell out during the night again.

***

It was a couple of years later, after that first camping episode. Sean's ingenuity and raw determination had served us well during those lean years after a business venture in Baker City failed. We not only were jobless and broke for a while, but also had to repay some expensive business debts. That didn't stop Sean from dreaming of owning a boat for fishing. He purchased an old wooden boat for thirty dollars, and proudly brought the thing home as if it were a trophy. I skeptically eyed the tattered vessel. Paint was peeling off; the wood looked rotten in places, and it was shallow and small. I told him that no way would I allow my children or myself in that boat on any body of water. "But look!" he exclaimed excitedly. "I can just sand down the boat, repair any bad places, refinish, and then it will be perfect!" His visionary and positive way of looking at potential opportunity was endless. How could I object? Besides, he had already bought the piece of junk and towed it home.

The boat took months of dedication and hard work. Painstakingly and lovingly, he worked the sander, bought repair parts and paint, and smoothed out the boat. Cassie helped in the process as well, learning a few wood-working skills. Sean had a dream for the boat that others would deem worthy only to burn or dispose of. Friends stopped by, smiled knowingly at me, and chuckled. Sean noticed, but he didn't care; and he didn't give up. Month after month he worked on it and researched what to do by going to marine stores and inquiring. Finally, after a year or so, he sealed, painted the boat, and was ready to launch it. He purchased an older used boat motor and some used cushions and life jackets. I bought a pet life vest for Penelope at a pet store, and we were all set to venture out on the water.

Sean launched the boat for its maiden voyage on a nearby lake, and we all joined him, wearing our life vests. Even Penelope was brought along for the first ride, just to get her accustomed to boating and water. She took it all in stride, overseeing her charges, Cassie and Jasmine. Penelope stationed herself at the front of the boat as lookout. The water was serene and calm, the boat easily floating along on the lake. Then we all spotted it at once, but Cassie called out, "Look Dad! What is it?"

Sean chuckled before answering. "You know that glass figurine your mom has on the piano? This is a real one—a dragonfly." We all exclaimed over its coloring—green, purple, navy, all reflecting from the sun on the water. All too soon, it flew away.

Sean's main goal for his boat was to launch it at the Washington coast and camp there. We loaded up the wooden boat, our pop-up camper and supplies, and headed over to the coast., near Ocean Shores. I drove the car, towing the camper, while Sean pulled the boat trailer using an older model Chevy pickup, the bed of it loaded with our supplies. We each had one child as a passenger, and Penelope rode with me. Somehow, we made it, usually at no more than thirty-five miles per hour. We set up camp, cooked hotdogs over the fire, and made plans for the next day.

First, we needed bait, which Sean knew how to find, so we made an outing out of it. Armed with a clam gun and shovel, we set out for the sandy beach of the nearby bay. As Sean shoved the clam gun into the sand and then brought it back up, the girls scrambled to burrow through the upturned sand, searching for sand shrimp. Penelope thought it great fun, and dug in the sand with her paw, too. Of course, she tried out the sand as a litter box, and then excitedly covered her deposit, digging down deeper than she had to.

"I got one!" Jasmine exclaimed, as a shrimp dangled in her hands.

"Quick, drop it in the bucket!" Sean said eagerly, and all of us looked for more. I usually pointed to a shrimp and one of the girls grabbed it. No way was I going to touch the squiggly thing. We continued until Sean decided that we had enough for bait.

We took our finds first to a jetty, where Sean and the girls fished with poles baited with the shrimp. They caught bullheads, a fish to use for crab bait. Now we had both crab bait with the bullheads, and shrimp to use as bait for fishing for salmon. After a quick lunch at the campsite, we loaded up crab nets into the boat, which Sean had already baited with the bullhead fish, fishing poles for salmon, and sand shrimp for baiting the poles. We scooped up Pens and were on our way. We launched and boarded the small wooden boat, setting out on the bay. The water greeted us in sparkling splendor, calm as glass, blue as the sky above. It was a glorious day to be on the water.

We trolled the bay, the boat motor in low gear, the boat gently floating on the water. Penelope wore her life vest and stood quivering at the front of the boat, looking out over the water. Her face looked anxious, but she didn't meow. We cast our crab nets for a couple of hours, circling back on each one to see if there were any keepers, and then recast again and again. We didn't get many nibbles from 'keepers,' which were the larger male crabs. "Time to bring in the crab nets and see what we can get on our fishing poles," Sean announced. As we slowly trolled on, he dangled his pole and one other for Cassie to keep an eye on. Slowly, we trolled farther and farther out, away from the familiar sights along the bay, and towards the bar. All that we had on board was the one solitary old boat motor, a coffee can to use for bailing excess water, a few snacks, and our floatable cushions and life jackets. We may have had a boat horn or flare, but I'm not sure. I noticed that Sean seemed to purposely steer the boat towards the bar which led to the open sea. "Where are we going?" I asked uneasily.

"Oh, don't worry. I know what I'm doing," he said, smiling confidently. The ancient boat motor sounded steady, but slowly and surely, the current was carrying us unmistakably out to the ocean. It was ominously silent now, except for the constant drone of the motor, which lugged down every time the boat took on a new roller wave. There we drifted, a sweet little family of four with a cat, heading out to try our luck at fishing in the Pacific Ocean. Our lives were dependent upon an old wooden boat, built for lake fishing, some thirty years ago. The children were unusually quiet as well, taking it in, trusting their Dad to keep them safe. Pens kept watch ahead but looked back at me occasionally, obviously wary at the turn of events. I felt helpless if anything went wrong. Before long, I could see the bar that we had left behind. The shoreline appeared miles away as we sat in the small, frail vessel.

"Mommy look!" Jasmine exclaimed in terror. The boat was floating in a violent swaying motion, and suddenly were lowered down between two huge waves. Water rose up on all sides as we sank into a swell about forty feet high. Then the boat rose up with the swell, and we could see the shore momentarily. Then we sank back down into the depths of the wave and could see only water on all sides. "Eeeeeeek!" Jasmine and I screamed together.

"Meowww!" Pens meowed piteously, getting down from her perch, and making her way over next to me, carefully stepping over a crab net. Stoically, Cassie sat there mute, scowling fiercely.

"Sean, what are we doing out here? Get us back now!" I roared. He just sat and grinned like a crazy man. I felt sick--but worse than that—I was terrified that we would all be drowned in the ocean and perish. I didn't see any other boat to rescue us. Reluctantly, Sean turned the boat back towards the bar, saying nothing. Slowly, the boat puttered its way back, the motor occasionally sputtering as it encountered a large wave. No one said anything now as all of us but Sean clung to the sides of the boat in silent terror. Penelope hunkered down by my feet. When we safely passed through the bar and back into the bay, I breathed a sigh of relief. However, I was angry at him for putting all of us at the mercy of the wooden boat. "What were you thinking bringing all of us out there?" I demanded.

"Oh, I knew the conditions were good. No worries." His grin looked maniacal and his eyes were glistening. I felt uneasy-- an alarm went off in my head.

Did I really know this guy? Did Sean even care about us and our safety at all? Did he actually bring us all out here on purpose for his own personal joy ride, risking our lives? I pondered these questions after the little boat entered the calm waters of the bay. I resolved that I would never let him do something like that with all of us again. I shuddered, hoping it was not a precursor to problems in the future as a family.

Twenty-four

"I believe cats to be spirits come to earth.
A cat, I am sure, could walk on a cloud
without coming through."

— Jules Verne (author, *Journey to the Center of the Earth*)

As it turned out, Penelope seemed to understand that food and essential expenses were more dear living in the Las Vegas area. Indeed, our move there had proven more expensive than we had expected. Prices for food and housing were higher than we had realized, at least in comparison to Sean's wages. I brought in a little money doing some freelance work, but not enough to make any big difference. Early one morning, not long after we had moved there, Cassie came rushing into my bedroom. "Mom—come quick! Pete isn't in his cage!"

Instantly, I was awake and threw on my bathrobe. "Okay, I'm coming!" I called back, padding down the hall after her. Since we were new to the Las Vegas area, we found different ways to entertain ourselves. One of them included buying a baby finch from our neighbor, who raised finches and other exotic birds. Then we bought a lovely decorator cage at a good price. The cage was an unusual charcoal color, made of shiny plastic, in the shape of a house, even with an opening that looked like a door. Every day I enjoyed listening to our little bird, Pete, sing. He lifted his head, opened his beak, and sang his little heart out. On this morning, all was strangely quiet.

I joined Cassie in the kitchen, where Pete's cage hung from the ceiling in the corner of the room. Sure enough, there was no Pete. "What in the world? Did anyone let Pete out?"

By now, Jasmine heard the commotion and toddled in to see what was going on. "Where's Pete?" she asked.

"That's what we want to know." Cassie nodded in agreement, her eye scanning the upper cabinets, searching for Pete. Sean had already left for work, so he wasn't available to ask for Pete's whereabouts. I made a careful inspection of the cage. The door was securely shut, and all the bars of the cage were undisturbed. Then, I looked down to the floor beneath the cage and noticed the tell-tale feathers. "Uh oh. I think that Pens somehow snagged Pete through the bars. I don't see how, though. See all the feathers down here?" I pointed to the feathers scattered on the floor--then we wandered into the next room. There, Penelope was carefully grooming herself, obviously just having enjoyed a succulent feast. There were more feathers in front of her, strewn on the floor. No one had fed her anything yet this morning; she had found her own breakfast inside the "decorator" cage. I marched over to her as she luxuriantly sat grooming herself. "Pens! Bad girl! You ate our sweet songbird!" Jasmine bent over, examining the feathers and burst into tears. Penelope merely kept licking each front paw meticulously, enjoying every delicious molecule of flavor, but looked up at us guiltily as we called out her name.

Jasmine continued to cry, while Cassie angrily glared at Pens, her eyebrows furrowed. "I hate that cat now."

"We mustn't blame Pens. She only did what her instincts told her to do. She is a born hunter of birds and mice. She saw her chance and took it." I felt sad, too, but at the same time, the whole thing took on a ludicrous, humorous note. Here I had purchased a very special cage that had bars spaced wide enough for our clever Pens to reach in and ensnare our innocent little songbird. The poor bird was doomed from the start. I felt guilt for not shopping for the correct cat-proof cage. Admittedly, I had found the cage in a furniture store, not a pet store--my mistake for sure. I managed not to laugh but continued putting on my sad face in front of the girls. I cleaned up the cage and donated it to Goodwill, hoping that the next bird owner didn't also own a precocious cat.

To console the girls, Sean and I agreed to bring home a hamster. We purchased a hamster cage from the pet store, confident that it would keep the hamster safe from our roaming predator, Penelope. We gave the girls strict instructions on keeping the door to the cage securely shut always, and to keep tabs on the hamster if they took it out to pet him. Cassie named the rodent Harry. Soon, Harry mysteriously let himself out at night after we were all sleeping, and then scurried back into his cage before daybreak. The door to the cage was firmly shut, but each night, somehow Harry let himself out to transfer his seed stash to a growing hoard pile inside a lower bathroom cabinet. Before we went to bed, we double-checked to make sure Harry's cage door was securely latched, but every morning, we saw that the hoard pile had gotten larger. Since Harry's cage was in Cassie's room, each morning she checked as soon as she awakened, only to find Harry snug inside his cage sleeping.

One night, things took a different turn. I went to sleep after having a late snack—a sandwich-- and left the empty plate on the floor beside me; it was empty except for a bit of lettuce left on the plate. I was awakened around two in the morning to a teeny nibbling sound—just barely audible. I roused sleepily, turning on the light, and there was Harry, chewing the leftover lettuce. He looked so cute, perched on the plate, nibbling away happily, until I chanced to glance into the doorway. There was Penelope, in full-crouch hunting position, just ready to spring. Her eyes were cold, steely, and fastened on little Harry. He was about to become her next snack. "Nooo!" I yelled, diving toward Harry to catch him in time. When I lunged, Pens sprang into action also, narrowly missing Harry. The plate slid into the wall on contact with Pens, clattering against it.

Sean awakened, complaining. "What's all the ruckus? Can't a guy get some sleep around here?" He sat up briefly, took in the scene before him: me holding onto a squirming Harry, and Pens still glaring at her prey from the doorway. "Oh my gosh! I don't believe this!"

He turned over and closed his eyes. As I scolded Penelope, I carried little Harry back to Cassie's room. Soon both girls heard the uproar and were wide awake. Jasmine looked at Pens accusingly, and Cassie bent over the cage, trying to see how Harry made his nightly jailbreaks. There was nothing to give any clue as to how he did it.

Harry's nocturnal raids to the bathroom cabinet continued, even after Cassie and I cleaned out his stash. The pile started over again, growing night by night. One morning, however, Cassie awoke to peer inside Harry's cage, and there was no Harry. We looked everywhere for three days, scouring every corner, every cabinet drawer, and behind all the furniture. No Harry. He just vanished, leaving no clue. We all assumed what had happened—Penelope had one more delicious feast and ate every morsel. The girls were disappointed and sad for about a week, refusing to pet Penelope, but then got over it after I donated yet another cage. We all agreed not to furnish Pens with any more delectable fresh snacks.

Soon after that incident, Sean announced that he was ready to quit the job in Las Vegas and move back home to Springville. It had been a somewhat difficult year anyway, and the girls and I were ready to go home too.

Twenty-five

1990

"Cats don't like change without their consent."

— Roger Caras

Moving became a way of life for us. We moved mostly for job changes or business ventures, but occasionally, to improve our housing situation. All of us became experts at how to downsize and pack our possessions. We started with three piles: one to throw out, one to give away, and a third to pack. As I looked back, it was a frenzied life style in comparison to my stable, predictable life later. At the time, the chaotic process of packing up all our belongings, renting moving trucks, and loading boxes and furniture seemed ordinary.

In 1990, we had moved from Springville, Washington, to Las Vegas for a job opportunity for Sean, to work with a friend and learn the automotive repair business. While we lived there that year, I did some free-lance writing for the community newspaper.

Penelope also became expert at moving, navigating each neighborhood. It took just two or three days of confinement indoors until she knew it was our new home, and then we released her outside. She understood our property boundaries, and we always found her waiting for us at the edge of our yard.

While living in Las Vegas for less than one year, we moved three times. The house prearranged for our arrival to Las Vegas was in a neighborhood with bars at the windows and doors; I felt as though I were living in a jail. We moved from there as soon as possible, to another rental in a better neighborhood. Soon after, our home in Washington sold, so we were free to purchase a home in Las Vegas, moving to a third house just outside the city in a nice suburb. Then the job Sean trained for didn't work out. I never knew why—Sean just shrugged his shoulders when I asked about it. Once more, we packed up, but this time, our destination was back to Washington.

Even though we had hoped for a future in Las Vegas, we were relieved to be returning to the Northwest. The endless, hot summer days were getting to all of us. One spring day, Jasmine came running into the kitchen, exclaiming, "Mommy, look! It's raining!" The girls and I ran outside, faces to the sky, trying to absorb what moisture would land on our faces and tongues.

Sean read in the newspaper of an existing auto repair business for sale in Springville. "This is my opportunity," Sean proclaimed. "We can return to Springville and I'll get a loan to buy the business." He grinned, obviously pleased with himself. I considered his idea, not sure what to think.

"Uh, I don't know, Sean. Sounds risky."

"I know I can do it. It'll be great--my own business!" Sean was emphatic. At least, we had a plan and he would create a job for himself—and we'd be back in Springville. It was all we had going for us, and I wanted to return home.

One more time the boxes came out, and we packed for the long journey home to Washington. While living in Las Vegas, we had barely scraped by, and our debts were accumulating. We asked my folks if we could live at their house until Sean could earn an income from the new business and our house in Nevada sold. It would also give us time to pay off the debts owed on credit cards.

Our new friends in Las Vegas helped us load up a huge U Haul truck for the move back home. Two of the guys helped Sean with loading my heavy Baldwin piano. The truck was not only the biggest I had ever seen, but the oldest, with six gears plus reverse. "I hope this beast will get us home," Sean said dubiously, eyeing the large vehicle.

"Me too. Plus, do you think I can drive it with all those gears?" I asked, examining the gearshift knob.

"Yeah, piece of cake," he said. We had to tow our car, an aging Datsun. This was to be Penelope's place to travel: we cracked the windows and put her litter box, food, and water in the back. This was before we knew about cat carriers. Penelope stood on her hind legs in the driver seat of the car to look out. Her face was wild with trepidation, the white on her face in stark contrast to her black head-- eyes wide. We scrambled into the truck; we would have to take turns on the three seatbelts the truck afforded, but began with the kids sharing one. There was barely room for the four of us, but it would have to do.

Our friends waved goodbye, promising to pray for our safe journey. With a lurch and a loud groan, the truck lumbered off with Sean at the wheel. Our friends laughed at the sight of Penelope peering out the windshield of the car; they continued waving and pointing at the cat as we rounded the corner, disappearing from them and our Nevada life forever.

The old truck roared down the freeway, bouncing all of us out of our seats occasionally. "This truck is awesome!" Cassie declared.

"I know!" Sean yelled in return so that Cassie could hear him above the din of the engine. "It's fun to drive, too!" The miles flew by. We were so excited to be heading back to Washington, that we stopped only for gas or restroom breaks, and bought food to eat on the road. We checked on Penelope during the stops; she seemed to be faring just fine. I took my turn at the wheel, becoming expert at going through the six gears in no time. It was exhilarating and fun! The highway was hot and dry in August--endless miles stretched behind and before us. We drove in the right-hand lane, since the truck was heavily loaded and towing the Datsun.

After several hours on the road, drivers began speeding around us and honking their horns, staring at us strangely as they whizzed by. Soon, the passengers in the cars seemed to be attempting to say something to us. "What's up with these people?" Sean complained. "Haven't they ever seen a U Haul towing a Datsun with a cat in it before?"

"I don't know--Nevada drivers, I guess. We're going the minimum speed, right?"

"Right."

Finally, one driver slowed down to our speed, keeping pace alongside the truck, the passenger lowering her window. Together, both driver and passenger yelled something at us. Then they sped on around our truck.

"What did they say?" Sean bellowed above the roaring truck. He looked at me, bewildered. I glanced back, clueless. The radio was blaring, and our windows were down, competing with the heat, making conversation nearly impossible.

"I don't know--something about tires," I yelled back.

"I think they said, 'your tires are on fire!'" Cassie shouted. Just at that instant, another driver attempted to signal us, his eyes wide in alarm, and then sped by.

"What do you suppose is going on?" I asked, perplexed. We all looked at one another in disbelief. No one said anything; the information from the other driver and passenger taking a few moments to dawn on us.

"What the heck?" Sean asked at long last. We decided to pull over to check just to be sure. It took several more miles to reach an off ramp and find a safe place to stop. We all leaped out quickly, eager for a chance to stretch our legs. While Sean and I meticulously inspected the truck tires, the children scampered back to the car to see Penelope. From Sean's and my vantage point, the small car wasn't visible.

"Dad! Mom! Quick!" Cassie cried out. We ran back behind the truck to the car, and there it was: the two front car tires were billowing smoke, ready to burst into flames at any moment. The tread was shredded and hanging in strips--steel belts exposed. Little was left that resembled tires. They would surely have ignited had we gone many miles farther. Worst of all, poor Penelope had one front paw on the driver door, and the other clung wildly to the steering wheel. Her face was panic stricken--her eyes, bulging and terrified.

"Poor Pens!" I exclaimed. We jerked the car door open and got her out, safely depositing her and her litter box into the cab of the truck. We surmised what had happened--the steering wheel had locked with Penelope pressing down on it. The tires had frozen into a braked position and were skidding down the road without revolving as Penelope held onto the wheel. We used the car key to unlock the steering wheel of the car. Fortunately, the off ramp led us a short distance into a town where we were able to find a tire store and buy tires. For that, and the fact that we stopped before a tire fire catastrophe, we breathed a prayer of thanks.

Soon we were on our way once more, bound for Washington, our cab fuller than before with four humans, a cat, and a litter box. Incidentally, Penelope was too stressed to use the litter box in the truck, but it was there in case. Anxious to arrive, Sean and I traded off driving the manual-shift truck, pushing on throughout the night and into the next day. We arrived at my parents' house exhausted, hot and sweaty, but very happy to be back. Temporarily, our home would be my folks'—and we hoped, not for very long.

Twenty-six

August 1991

"A cat has absolute emotional honesty: human beings, for one reason or another, may hide their feelings, but a cat does not."

— Ernest Hemingway (author, *For Whom the Bell Tolls*)

Mom was overjoyed to see us and have us stay—Dad, not so much. I saw his grim countenance as the monstrous U Haul truck pulled into the driveway in front of his tidy garage. Up until that point, Dad had a place for everything; he practically used a card catalog for where all his tools and accessories were assigned. All our earthly possessions were dumped into his garage, including Penelope and her litter box; Dad's private sanctuary was destroyed.

Dad didn't like cats inside, whether they be in the house or garage. He forbade Penelope to be in the house, so her living quarters had become his garage. I noticed him staring grudgingly at Pen's litter box, which he claimed smelled horrid, even if I had just cleaned it.

We all tried to adjust to living under one roof. Things seemed to take on a little routine, but I knew Dad was barely tolerating the situation with Penelope. Since Penelope had to remain in the garage, I visited her there. I often found her watching Dad while he worked on endless carpentry projects at his workbench. He suddenly seemed obsessed with building birdhouses. I sensed that it was stressful for him to have the four of us under foot in his once quiet home, and he sought out the garage as refuge, only to find Penelope there.

It was clear that the two, Dad and Penelope, didn't particularly like one another. From inside the house, I could hear Dad running his power saw or hammering on some piece of wood. Every so often I went out to check on Penelope, who must have been stressed with all the mechanical noise. I found her glowering at Dad from the top of a stack of boxes, her facial expression stern. "That cat is always staring at me," Dad complained, continuing to work feverishly at his workbench, his work area hemmed in by our maze of boxes.

Suddenly, Penelope's eyes narrowed to pin point slits as she focused on the floor just inside the garage door. She assumed a cautious, crouched position, moving ever so slowly, almost unnoticed by the naked eye, until she sprang into action. Just like that, she nailed a mouse as it dared to venture in from under the garage door. Dad stopped his hammering, his arm poised in midair, watching in utter amazement. Penelope proudly carried her prey in her mouth to a remote corner, where she played with it, paralyzed and killed it, and then ate it.

"Heh, heh. That was great!" Dad exclaimed, smiling broadly. "It's a good thing Penelope was in here to get the mouse before it set up a nest."

"I know. She's good," I said, pleased at his compliment.

"Well, she can stay in my garage anytime." Dad shook his head in wonder, continuing his work. Another of Penelope's skills had come in handy that day. She seemed to know how to make herself useful and get on the good side of everyone—including Dad.

We would need that to get through the months of living with my parents until Sean obtained and established his auto repair business. Our family required more income to change all of that.

Twenty-seven

1993

"Tully, I discovered a great housing market in Baker City. I want us to move there to begin my contractor business next month—in July." Sean looked over at me from across the dinner table expectantly with an inane grin. We finally had a little stability, living in our new home, just purchased a year ago, and Sean seemed to be doing well with his automotive repair business. I deliberately set my fork down, breathing in deeply, forcing myself not to explode with emotion. I really couldn't take in what I had just heard him say.

"What are you saying?" My voice betrayed me; it rose to a hysterical level. Jasmine picked up on the tone.

"What's wrong, Mommy?" Her eyes held mine in fear; picking up on my bristling at Sean's declaration.

"It's okay, Jasmine. Finish your meal and go play." I stared hard at Sean, trying to convey that this was not the time or place to break such news. Cassie absently toyed with her food.

"Can I be excused?" Cassie asked. She still had sight in only the one eye but caught on fast when it came to visual cues.

"Sure. You too, Jasmine. Pick up your plates and put them in the sink." It was only after they left the room that I allowed myself to exhale. "What in the world? What are you talking about? Are you crazy? A month? What were you thinking?" I couldn't help myself. It all spilled out in an angry rush. As I flooded the air with my questions,

Penelope heard the timbre, and slowly sauntered over to my chair. She, too, looked up in alarm, knowing instinctively that something affecting her family was being discussed. She brushed up against my leg, meowing as if to ask if I was okay. I petted her head absently. "It's okay, Pens. Thanks for checking on us." She seemed satisfied but sat down just a short way from my chair just in case. Her ears were fully pricked, listening. I drew in my breath before saying, "Tell me all about it. But be sure of one thing—the three of us and Pens can't move that soon. We only moved from my folks' house last year."

"Well, that's okay. Maybe I can go there first and get things started. I could even get a rental house in Baker City lined up. It's too early to purchase one; we need to sell here first of course. Maybe we need to see how it goes for a while anyway." Sean grinned ridiculously again, which only made me feel like I couldn't trust this man, or this move to work out. *Why did I always have to follow him and his crazy ideas around and leave my reporting job?* I resisted the urge to say that and took a sip of coffee instead.

"Go on—I'll listen." As he chatted away excitedly, I got the main drift. He had been increasingly dissatisfied with his work in automotive repair and had recently gotten his contractor's license. Naively, I was all for it at the time, not realizing he would suddenly want to leave the area, sell the business and house and start over again. We had returned from the move to Nevada just two years ago. Besides, I was enjoying Springville again, happily returning to my newspaper job, and Cassie was doing well in school here. I was planning to enroll Jasmine in kindergarten for the fall. All of that changed with Sean's latest scheme to start a construction business in the up-and-coming Eastern Washington town of Baker City.

Once we moved to Baker City, I planned to ask the paper if I could do feature stories from there and email them in. Otherwise, I would have to forget my own career again. I hoped they would accept at least some of my work from out of town.

Penelope knew the moving routine well by this time, and once we arrived, she again learned to navigate the new neighborhood within just a couple of days. Cassie and Jasmine loved our new home, a rental situated on an acre of land. The girls spent the remainder of the summer exploring for lizards and scorpions and observing jack rabbits. Sean hired extra help after just two months, when it became too much for one person to keep up. Within a year, however, he found out that his foreman was stealing lumber and supplies from him and running a business on the side.

Sean's construction business went bankrupt quickly, and we had to pack up and return to our secure haven in Springville once more-- really broke this time. Now, Sean had no business, no job prospects, plus he owed back business taxes. I could still get occasional feature story assignments, but that would pay for only food and a portion of rent. *What were we going to do?* I was angry that Sean had allowed his foreman to steal from him. *Why didn't he check up on his employees?* He trusted people to a fault—so now we were in this mess. Angrily, I threw our belongings into cardboard boxes once more. It crossed my mind that I should just leave this man. Then I reminded myself that I had no real job either. *How would we ever dig our way out of the debt? Was I doing right by my children to stay with him? How would we pay off the debt and yet provide for our family?* I had so many doubts—so many unanswered questions.

Again, Penelope stood next to me and watched, knowing what was coming--another move. She would do her best to help us as our little nanny cat. "I know you want to help, Pens. Just being here when I'm down helps a lot." I patted her head while she purred in reply, her rhythmic sound comforting me. I managed to say a silent prayer, asking God to help us get through this hard time and still stay together. There weren't any other options.

Twenty-eight

1994

"Time is for dragonflies and angels. The former live too little and the latter live too long."

— James Thurber

I resented Sean for allowing his employee to steal from him. The bankruptcy, with all the legal process and expense, seemed needless and foolish to me. I had gone along with the business only because I had to and moving to Baker City and back added to my bitterness. We returned to Springville and found a rental to move into. It was near the neighborhood where Cassie had attended school before., and now both girls were in school. Life returned to normal as much as possible. I took on more assignments from the paper, and at least, I was back in the local area.

All my ill feelings were forgotten when Sean complained of pain in his groin area and needed immediate surgery for a double hernia repair. When he was discharged from the hospital, I drove him home, trying not to veer into any potholes in the road. Every bump or turn made him groan with discomfort. I set Sean up in his easy chair in the family room, and he winced, grabbing at the site of the incision. "What channel do you want to watch on T.V.?" I asked, attempting to get his mind off his pain.

"ESPN Sports," he answered, grimacing. During the days which followed, I helped him to the bathroom, the shower, and changed the bandages. Then there were the three meals to prepare for him each day, and the endless supply of beverages to carry to him while he sat helpless in his chair. The surgery took a while to heal, since it was a deep incision, and with the discomfort, Sean became more disagreeable and hard to please. It was even difficult for him to stand up. I waited on him constantly, unless I was away on assignment. I tried to get him to eat balanced meals, but when I wasn't around, I knew he ate junk food, some of which he stashed in hiding spots. In a twisted irony, Sean and I drew closer in our relationship. He needed me, and I enjoyed catering to him.

We owned three cats at the time: Penelope, Ginger, and Paddy. They all got along fine and seemed to enjoy hunting outside together. While Sean recuperated from surgery, the three cats tried to cheer him up by bringing home trophies in the early morning. One such morning, I awakened, went out on the back deck, and there the trophies were lined up in a perfect row: two mice and a dragonfly. I could've used a ruler and they wouldn't have been more evenly spaced. I knew Paddy was the one who brought in the dragonfly. He was such a little cat, and it was the best he could do. I walked back into the house to report to Sean, who still sat in the easy chair twenty-four hours a day while he was recovering. "Sean, each of the cats brought you a present—two mice and a dragonfly."

"Heh, heh. Those darn cats," he chuckled, wincing at the effort to laugh a little. "You know, they do help take my mind off the pain for a minute or two." I assisted Sean to get up out of the chair to hobble out onto the deck to see the lineup of gifts. It was a very comical sight--one that I will always remember.

Around this same time, Penelope developed an infection, probably from encountering a strange cat in our yard and fighting to defend her territory . I took her to the vet, who prescribed antibiotic pills for her, to be given two times per day. Sean also took antibiotics two times a day for his surgical incision. I placed Penelope's pills on a separate shelf to keep her meds from Sean's supply. One day, Sean found the cat meds, shook out two to take with his water. "Stop!" I yelled as he held the pills to his open mouth.

"What?" He frowned at me—irritated at the interruption. The pills dropped onto his tongue, but he hadn't swallowed yet.

"Those belong to Pens!" I snatched the water glass from his hand, so he wouldn't take a sip and swallow the pills.

"Great. I nearly took cat pills. Doctors would have had to pump my stomach. Keep those stinkin' things away from me in a better hiding spot," he grumbled.

"That's why I keep her pills here on this shelf. Yours are by your chair inside the table drawer." I chuckled a little at his exaggeration, trying to humor him back into a good mood.

The day arrived when Sean went to the doctor to see if he had healed completely. He was hopeful, but the doctor said the surgery would take another month to heal on the inside. He would not be able to lift anything more than ten pounds until then.

Not only did I care for two patients at once—Sean and Pens—but ironically, later, also two eye surgery patients at once: Cassie and Bear, a cat we adopted later. Our Bear cat, a black Manx with a stub tail, ran into the fence outside and broke his eye open. After Bear's eye surgery, I had to put drops in his eye four times a day and assist Cassie with her eye drops six times a day. At one point, Cassie nearly made the same mistake with cat eye drops as Sean did with cat pills. "What the heck?" Cassie complained. "I thought these were my eye drops, not Bear's." I grabbed the cat eye drops from out of her hand before she applied them to her eye.

"Yeah, well, I have these on this shelf. Your drops are on your bed table, remember?" I was beginning to have an idea of what a nurse must feel like with my patients, humans and cats. Life with cats had its moments. Eventually, Sean returned to work, but limited his lifting for several months.

Twenty-nine

1994

> *"I regard cats as one of the great joys in the world. I see them as a gift of the highest order."*
> — Trisha McCagh

We adopted Paddy as a kitten while living in Baker City, around the same time as our cat, Ginger, but from different litters. Paddy was the classic Garfield, a bright orange tabby--his stripes beautifully highlighted in white. He loved to eat, snuggle with us, and purr. He endeared everyone to him and was the most docile, easy going cat I ever lived with.

It was little wonder, then, that the children loved playing with Paddy or "Pads," often dressing him up in clothes. They entered him in a pet costume contest, dressing him as a bandit, complete with a mask, shirt, toy gun, and a name badge that said, "Pads: Bad to the Bone." It was a humorous irony that made everyone who saw it chuckle. Affectionate Pads was anything but "bad to the bone."

Paddy harbored no ill will to any human or cat; he just ambled along through life, assuming everyone else felt the same way. It was with horror and disbelief when he came into the house one day, seriously injured by someone. "Mom! Come see Paddy!" Jasmine cried out. I dropped what I was doing and found the girls crouched down by the cat, listening to his horribly labored breathing. His sides heaved terribly as he gasped for air.

"Who did this?" I asked more to myself than the children. Immediately, I rushed him to the vet before leaving for work. I left him there in the care of the vet, who said he would get back to me on the diagnosis as soon as possible. It wasn't long before I got the phone call: Paddy had been maliciously kicked in the side, dislodging his diaphragm, thus making his breathing extremely difficult and painful. *Who would do such a cruel thing to such a harmless, lovable animal?* We allowed our cats to go outside, and even though Pads never went very far, he did go a little past our yard and into the neighborhood. I pondered this as I drove back to the vet as soon as I could break away from the newspaper office.

When I returned to the vet, I had to make a quick and difficult decision to either have him euthanized as soon as possible or undergo a risky and expensive surgery to repair Paddy's diaphragm. The vet cautioned that the surgery might not even help. I called Sean— regretfully, we opted to put Paddy down. I saw him one last time, gasping for air, his beautiful orange and white stripes turned to a sickly brown and white color, probably due to his pain. I bade him a tearful goodbye. It was horrible to see him in that state, but I reassured myself that we had done the best we could.

Sean came home later that evening and we all sat around, tearfully recounting the most loveable cat we ever had. "Well, I think you should call the vet in the morning and ask for Paddy's body. I'll pick it up on my way home tomorrow and bury him in our yard. Then he will always be close to us."

I had been in such a distressed state at the vet's, I hadn't thought to ask for Paddy's body. I was taken back at his thoughtfulness. "I'm so glad you thought of that. Thank you, Sean," I answered softly, smiling through tears.

"Of course. Pads is part of the family," he said gently. The girls also seemed relieved at the thought of having Paddy buried close at hand. It was a comforting gesture for all of us, somehow helping us cope with the cruel act that brought about our sweet cat's demise.

When Sean offered to return Paddy home to his final resting place, I saw a glimpse of his gentleness. We always agreed in our love of felines. At least we still had that in common, no matter what other problems that came between us.

Thirty

1994

"Cats choose us; we don't own them."

— Cristin Cast

"Here Ginger, kitty, kitty," I called out. Either Jasmine or I had been calling out to Ginger every day for the past month. Our elusive, beautiful tortoise shell cat was missing, and Jasmine was heartbroken. So, we kept trying to lure her home, but so far, no cat. It was pitch black by this time of evening, and Sean had just driven into the driveway, arriving home from work with take-out. He got out of the car holding a bag of burgers for our dinner. He found us on the step, calling out for Ginger, as we had been doing every evening. It seemed a useless exercise by now, but for Jasmine's sake, we kept trying.

Opening the bag, Sean raised his voice saying, "Here Ginger girl," while waving the meat-fragrant sack aloft into the air. I thought to myself that it was a futile gesture. However, as the wind carried the rich, meat aroma, out of nowhere, a cat emerged. It was so dark out, that our eyes seemed to be playing tricks. *Was there really a cat? Could it be Ginger?* I tried to focus my eyes in the darkness. Yes, there she was-- it was unbelievable but true! There was Ginger, just waiting to be enticed and plied with food. Eagerly, the cat began wolfing down the burger patty feast set before her on the porch.

"Wow! Why didn't we think of smelly meat before?" I asked. Sean opened another burger wrapper and set it down with a grin, very satisfied that he had been the one to bring Ginger running.

Jasmine looked at the cat suspiciously, shaking her head in disbelief. "That's not Ginger. Ginger is smaller than this cat; she looks way different from this one."

"No, it's Ginger," Sean insisted. I agreed. "She's just gotten bigger and older since she went missing.

"Are you sure? It just doesn't look like my Ginger."

"Jasmine, remember the last time she disappeared? You barely recognized her then, too," I recalled. We all remembered. We feared that she had been run over or some such tragedy had befallen our cat. In fact, Ginger had disappeared more than once.

***

A while before this, Ginger had been gone three days when we heard a muffled sound overhead. "Do you hear something?" I had asked that morning.

"No, only the wind," Cassie had said.

Jasmine listened carefully, cocking her head from side to side. "No, I don't hear anything."

"Come this way, out to the family room area," I directed. We kept turning our heads, trying to hear even the faintest sound. There it was again—an unmistakable meowing sound.

"I hear it! It's Ginger!" Jasmine declared, jumping up and down with excitement. The meowing was coming from the attic. We had to wait for Sean to get home, so he could bring a ladder to go up and retrieve her. We never did figure out for sure how our cat had gotten into the attic. The rental house was in disrepair--not a very nice place to live. There were holes in the walls; perhaps Ginger had found a way to the attic through a small opening somewhere. Also, the furnace didn't work; we heated the house with a small woodstove, which warmed only the living room and kitchen. Sean had looked for work for months after we returned from the business failure in Baker City, until he landed another job at a warehouse. I was able to return to the newspaper reporting job part time. Those were the lean years of our family, but we pushed through.

The first time Ginger vanished, she was gone only one day. Our neighbor had heard a meowing sound under the hood of his car as he drove to his workout. Two hours later as he traveled home, he heard the sound again. He looked under his car and there was Ginger. She had managed to ride to the gym and back home again, clinging to the undercarriage of the car.

After we again moved the following year, Ginger vanished forever. Somehow even Jasmine grew to understand her cat's yearning to wander and accepted the fact that she would never return.

Thirty-one

Jasmine
1998

We've been sitting here in the waiting room since eight this morning. There's a clock overhead and it shows ten o'clock. Cassie is in surgery again-- I've lost track of how many times she has had an eye operation. Mom makes me come along every time. I bring a book and a puzzle, but it's always the same: boring. Why can't I stay home by myself now? I'm ten years old and perfectly capable. Besides, the cats are home to keep me company. Dad drove here separately so he can jet off to work as soon as Cassie goes into recovery. He looks bored, too, and keeps falling asleep in front of the waiting room TV. No wonder—all that's on is one of those cooking shows.

Mom is sitting on the edge of her chair. She is always nervous and worried when we have to go to these surgeries. She's staring at the double doors leading into the operation room, like she is really wanting to go in there. The nurse said that we all must wait out here. Guess I'll read my book for a while, but I get tired of just sitting. At home, I could play with Penelope or Paddy or watch nature shows. I would like to be home practicing my piece for the next piano recital. Cassie takes all our energy and time, and I'm sick of it.

Plus, after each surgery, we must take Cassie in for follow up exams with her doctor. Again, I always have to tag along. When will this all end?

Thirty-two

"Never try to out stubborn a cat."
— Robert A. Heinlein, *Time Enough for Love*

My love affair with Manx cats began when Cassie called from a fund-raising event at school. "Mom, there's a little black kitten here that my friend Jessica brought. Her mom won't let her keep the kitten--can I bring it home?" When I hesitated, she continued. It's all black and has just a tiny nub of a tail. So cute!"

"Well, we already have two cats. What do we need with a third?" I asked, trying to be objective, but at the same time, feeling the pull to allow her to bring home an adorable kitten. At this time, we still had Paddy, and of course, Penelope.

"Who is it?" Sean wanted to know. He was watching football on T.V.

I held my hand over the receiver of the phone. "It's Cassie. She has a kitten with no tail and wants to bring it home." I shook my head no at him.

"Is it a Manx?" Sean asked, perking up from the football game, suddenly interested in my conversation with Cassie. "Ask her if male or female," he added, his eyes riveted to the phone. Exasperated, since I didn't really want a third cat, I asked Cassie if male or female. Jessica thought female but wasn't sure. "Well, it's got to be a Manx, so tell her to bring it home," Sean instructed. I recalled then when Sean once told me about owning Manx cats as a boy and enjoying their crazy antics and energy. So I knew the kitten's homelessness was at an end.

Cassie brought the kitten home in a small cardboard box. The kitten was a mere wisp of a cat--so tiny, fluffy, and adorable with just a hint of a tail with longer tufts of fur at the bottom end. We came up with the name Bear; she looked like a little black panda bear, all rounded curves: head, rump, tail, and short, compact body. I fell in love with the kitten right from the start. Bear, as with all kittens, was robust and full of energy. I tried keeping her in the house to become totally an indoor cat, but she pawed frantically at the door to be let out like my other two cats, Paddy and Penelope. Soon Bear found a way to climb up onto the top of the rooftop of the house, surveying every peak and view that the roof afforded. I learned later, from the veterinarian, that Manx cats are born climbers and jumpers, using their extra large hind legs. More importantly, though, the vet told me when I took Bear for her first shots, that she was a *he*, not a *she*.

Since Bear begged to go outside with the "big cats." I worried about such a small kitten getting lost. I put a small collar on him with Paddy's ID from the local animal shelter, since Bear was too young to have his own. Paddy didn't need it, since he always stayed close to home.

Bear loved to head out to the garage when Sean and Cassie worked on Cassie's car engine, an old Chevy. Every day after school, the three of them could be found out there, with Cassie working, Sean supervising, and Bear, the kitten, watching it all. The banging and machine noises didn't seem to faze the little cat; in fact, Bear seemed to like the loud commotion. As the weeks wore on, the engine project continued. I could always find Bear in the garage.

One evening after the work stopped for the day, I couldn't find Bear--this was unusual. I called him repeatedly. "Bear, here kitty." No Bear. I called him all through the evening, walking around our yard and up and down the street. No Bear. I even looked on the busy road behind our house to be sure he wasn't run over. The search continued day after day for three days. No Bear. We had all grown to love the little black fur ball with just a nub of a tail.

Just when I had almost given up, the phone rang. "Hello?" I answered.

"Are you Tully? This is John at Eastside Dodge. I have your cat, Paddy, here in our mechanic garage. He's been hanging out here in our garage all day, and we noticed that he is wearing an ID tag from the animal shelter. I called them, and they gave me your number."

Paddy is right here in the house, I'm thinking to myself, glancing over at him peacefully sleeping on the rug. "Oh, are you sure it's Paddy?" I asked, thinking there must be a mistake from the shelter.

"That's what the shelter said, and I have him right here. Black cat, right?" John asked.

Then I remembered. I had used Paddy's tag on Bear. "Oh, right! I'll be down to pick him up in five minutes! Thank you, thank you! By the way, his name is really Bear." I hung up quickly, told everyone, and jumped into my car, anxious to reach the kitten with the mistaken identity. As I drove, I felt thankful that I had thought to put the incorrect ID on Bear, never really thinking that I would need it.

The young man who called was very kind, smiling proudly as he handed Bear over to me. "I can hardly believe how your little cat wants to be in our noisy mechanic shop. He's some cat!" I explained how Bear loved being in our garage at home when Cassie and Sean were working on the Chevy engine. Somehow, Bear had traveled over three miles from home, wandering down a busy road, and heard the mechanic noises. Perhaps he thought it was our garage and walked inside. How he navigated all the traffic without getting run over was a total mystery. The pads of his tiny feet were calloused from the trek

We were thankful Bear knew to seek help in the mechanic garage—an unlikely place for a small kitten. Right away, I ordered a correct ID tag for him, but until it arrived, he continued to wear the one with the wrong identity.

***

Early on, Sean trained Bear to like water and to swim by dropping him into our bath tub. "He's going to learn to ride in my boat," Sean proclaimed. Bear got his "sea legs," becoming our dog-cat. He swam and wore a life vest made to fit his small size, and rode happily with us on our boat. By this time, Penelope was too elderly for such adventures. While boating, we also stayed in campgrounds, which Bear took to easily, walking on a leash. One time he got loose, and I thought we'd lost him forever.

"Bear, where are you? Here, kitty kitty," I called, a terrible lump forming in my throat, thinking he was truly gone. Plus, it was almost dark, nearly impossible to see a black cat. Suddenly, Cassie spotted the cat, high up on a tree branch.

"There he is, Mom!" Cassie shouted and pointed to where he was sitting on a branch.

"Run get his food dish," Sean commanded. "I'll stay here and talk to him." When I brought back the food, it worked; Bear came down and Sean grabbed him quickly.

Vet visits were unique with Bear. He visited there, not in a cat carrier like all other cats, but on his leash, strolling into the office ever so proudly. The office workers, doctors, and other pet owners chuckled, casting admiring glances Bear's way. He didn't mind the attention given him; in fact, he enjoyed every minute there--except for the shots.

Bear maintained high energy, running pell-mell into things, and scrambling to the roof top of the house, even after he reached maturity. One morning, after I had let him out, Bear must have run into the fence. I found him sitting there, his eye bleeding profusely. "Oh Bear! What happened to you?" I cried in dismay. I was on my way out to work that morning. I could see that his eye had been seriously injured, so I called in to my office to say that I had an emergency and would be late. I bundled Bear up in a blanket and hurried to a vet hospital.

The doctor there examined Bear's eye, saying, "Well, he needs eye surgery to repair his eye. I'm not sure he'll be able to see out of it again, but we will do our best. Actually," he continued, "I'm not even sure how well he ever saw anyway. For a cat to run into something, he may have been blind to begin with." What a thought; maybe that's why Bear always ran headlong into life, almost crazed.

Bear underwent an experimental eye surgery and the vet used his case in a study for other veterinarians. Because of this, the doctor only charged a fraction of the actual costs in surgery and follow-up visits. We got our sweet and crazy Bear back, but he had to endure many check-ups. Sometimes I had to bring Bear to work to fit in all the vet appointments. The other reporters loved his office visits. He seemed to fit right in, proudly ambling around the office while I worked.

Bear never got over his frantic desire to be allowed outside, no matter how hard I tried to keep him in. One fateful morning as I let him out, I had a bad feeling about it, but he was insistent, pawing at the door. It was too early—I was sleepy--and didn't want to be bothered. About an hour later, when I couldn't return to sleep, I got up, put on my robe, and went to the door. "Bear, here kitty, kitty," I called over and over. I had a terrible sense of foreboding as I walked out to the busy road behind our house. I found him on the road dead—still warm. He couldn't even see well enough to notice the car that hit him. He looked like he was asleep, with only a small place on his skull where he was struck. I picked him up, sobbing, my heart breaking. *I let him out,* I kept thinking in my head, blaming myself for this. I carried him in my arms to show Sean and the girls. The girls came outside in their pajamas, crying softly while Sean dug a hole in our back yard to put our dear Bear in the ground close to where Paddy was buried. Sean carried him to the hole, cradling the furry little body like a baby. I knew that Sean loved this cat as much as any of us did. *Why had I allowed him outside when I sensed the danger?* I asked myself this over and over. Bear was the last of my many cats I ever allowed to venture outdoors alone. From then on, no matter how persistently they demanded to go out, I made our cats become indoor only pets.

Thirty-three

2000

> *"Cats are intended to teach us that not everything in nature has a function."*
>
> — Garrison Keillor

It's true, the vet had warned me that perhaps Bear had been blind from birth, even before his eye injury and surgery. If he was indeed blind, he wouldn't have seen the car approaching that hit and killed him. As I carried that blame around day after day; Sean advised me to not dwell on it--there was nothing more to do about it. However, in my mind, I kept reliving the morning Bear was run over. I kept asking myself, *why had I let him out?*

After a month or two, I was able to put the feeling aside, and began searching for another Manx kitten. It had to be a male, like Bear, and preferably, dark in color. I called several leads for Manx cats, until at last, I found a breeder in the area. The woman said, "Yes, I have four kittens; two as yet are unspoken for." I could visit them and choose one, but the kittens weren't ready to be weaned for another month.

"Mom, are you ready to go with me to see some cute Manx kittens?" Cassie and Jasmine were in school, and I didn't want to wait. Mom agreed to go, and we set out the next morning, driving out on a country road. We passed by a covered bridge, and located the home, nestled on a hill overlooking the valley. The woman, named Louise, who bred Manx cats greeted us warmly. She explained that the mother cat was her indoor-outdoor pet, and she led us into her kitchen. There, in a little playpen, was the mother, a brownish color cat, and her four kittens. Three of her kittens were orange and white, and one was a black and brown tabby, with a crook in the tiny nub of a tail. "I love the little dark male," I said, wishing I could scoop him up and take him home. "Is he spoken for?"

"No, but you have to wait, and come back for him in a month. Manx kittens take longer to mature than other cats, and I have to make certain that they're all healthy," Louise said. "Here, you may hold him," she said, picking up the wee thing and handing him to me. I held him close, hoping to bond with him even in that moment. Louise took us on a tour of her cattery in a separate building. She pointed out the handsome father of the kittens, an orange tabby. I peeked in at him—he was stocky, no tail at all, which breeders call a "rumpy"— quite the handsome tom. Louise taught us more about the Manx cat, revealing her many years of expertise. She seemed so in awe of the Manx, respecting the complexities of reproducing this ancient breed. When we drove back to Springville, I could hardly wait for the time when I could return to get the little male kitten.

When Mom and I returned a month later, the kittens had doubled in size. I brought a cardboard box to transport the kitten. Louise provided a new, aqua colored baby blanket for his ride, and tears formed in her eyes as she lovingly placed first the blanket, and then the kitten, into the box. At that moment, I realized that she had wanted to keep him for herself. I hugged her in understanding, and promised to always care for him. "Please bring him back if he doesn't work out," she begged.

"Of course. But I love him already," I assured her. We were both crying by now, and I waved goodbye, my precious little cargo in the backseat of the car.

We named the kitten Nigel. Even though Penelope came and went at will outdoors, Nigel, I determined, would only be indoors unless on a leash. Nigel, typical of a Manx, climbed up onto shelves and cupboards, leaping off tall heights. When I took him to the vet for a checkup, the vet discovered an abdominal hernia which required an operation. Recovery from surgery meant absolutely no climbing and jumping for an entire month. I removed all the furniture from the spare bedroom where Nigel would have to be confined. This was difficult, as Nigel was very social. To keep him company, I slept in there with him by night for a month, and went in during the day to read, do office work, or watch TV. Sometimes Cassie or Jasmine took my place at night, so we alternated the sleep arrangements. Nigel had to have the surgery two more times before the hernia healed completely. Each time, one of us spent the night with him on a mat on the floor. Nigel bonded with each of us from our overnight stays in the spare bedroom with him, and he became a special addition to the family.

For spring break, the girls and I plus Nigel were making a trip to eastern Washington to visit my cousin, Veronica, who lived on a twenty-acre mini farm. Veronica owned several horses, chickens, a dog, and a cow. She had been inviting us to drive out for several years, and this time, we were finally going. Veronica didn't own a cat, and invited us to bring Nigel, who loved riding in the car. He would stay in Veronica's large farmhouse with us. Sean remained at home to work—I had a fleeting thought that maybe he would cheat on me while I was away. I put the doubt aside as the girls eagerly looked forward to our trip . Veronica promised that Cassie and Jasmine could ride her horses on the wooded trails behind her property. I might ride with them. With that happy thought, I pushed aside my fears about what Sean would do while I was away and prepared to go.

Off we started on the three-hour drive, with Nigel riding free range in the car. He loved to sit on my lap as I drove and look out the side window—this was before cat carriers. After two hours of travel, as we wound along the sharp curves of the mountainous highway, Nigel needed to use the litter box. "Mom, Nigel needs to go but it's too curvy for him to balance in the litter box. Pull over,'" Cassie demanded. Nigel meowed loudly, but I kept to the narrow, winding road, realizing there was nothing to be done about it—there was nowhere to pull over.

"I know—I can hear him!" I answered, continuing to drive. "There's nowhere to pull over—it's too narrow on the shoulder of the road." He clung precariously to my sleeve, refusing to leave my lap. "I have to keep driving." Cassie tried to coax him off my lap, but to no avail. Poor Nigel went number two on my arm, clinging to me wildly. I just kept driving, erratically now, with excrement on my arm, and a cat clinging to me with his claws, as the car swung wildly around the numerous curves.

"Ew, Mom!" Jasmine exclaimed. "Nigel just went on your arm and it stinks!"

"This is horrible! Ew! Pull over!" Cassie agreed.

"I know, I know. I'm right here!" Up ahead, a road crew stopped me; they had been painting a yellow line down the center of the road, which I had not noticed until that moment. One of the workers pulled me over, glaring at me angrily, and motioned for me to roll down my window. I heard him, through the closed window, asking, "Why are you purposely ruining our freshly painted line?

I can't roll down my window to talk, I thought. *I am too embarrassed.* Feces stuck to my arm, and Nigel planted his sharp nails into my shirt, still clinging to me. *The man will notice what's on my arm, and smell it,* I reasoned. Shaking my head no, I drove off. "Mom! Why didn't you answer him?" Cassie demanded. "I can't believe it." She rolled down her window for fresh air, but we traveled on until reaching Veronica's. We all got out, and I shook off the poop on my arm. Veronica stared at me, at first, not saying anything. Then she burst out laughing.

"What in the world?" She looked to me for explanation, but I just shook my head. Cassie and Jasmine filled her in on our ride with Nigel through the mountains.

We all had a great time in the country, including Nigel, our neurotic, fun-loving Manx cat. He delighted in exploring every nook and cranny in Veronica's big house, including climbing up on top of her kitchen cabinets and staring down at us. Veronica didn't mind— she was an animal lover. As we drove back home two days later on the same winding road, we all laughed at the swerving, erratic yellow lines that Nigel and I had created. Shortly after that trip, I bought a carrier for Nigel to ride in while traveling.

Arriving home, my heart sank when I saw that Sean's car wasn't in the driveway. He should have been home by that time, since it was already past eight in the evening. "Where's Dad?" Cassie asked, seeming to pick up on my sense of foreboding.

"Oh, you know. He always works late these days," I chirped, attempting levity. Jasmine bolted from the car and ran inside first, checking the sofa in the family room for signs of her dad.

"He hasn't been here at all. Everything looks like it did when we straightened up before leaving," Jasmine proclaimed.

"He's just been busy working," I insisted, not believing a word.

"Right. Sure Mom," Cassie said, giving me a sideways knowing look. I said no more and just began unloading our bags, but first set Nigel down in the house to roam around and check on Penelope and Susie, our third cat at that time. Neither Pens nor Susie liked riding in the car, and we left them at home with an automatic feeder-- I didn't trust Sean to remember to feed them. I passed Penelope, who lay on Jasmine's bed and I headed to my bedroom. Susie lay sprawled on my bed, looking up at me lazily when I brought in my bag. We had recently adopted Susie, a beautiful black Manx.

"Susie, I wish you could tell me what happened while we were gone." She trilled a little and stretched. Pens couldn't say anything either. I had to go on my instincts.

Thirty-four

2001

"I have studied many philosophers and many cats. The wisdom of cats is infinitely superior."

— Hippolyte Taine

After Sean's business in Baker City had gone bankrupt, we returned to Springville, in debt and jobless. We were required to repay a portion of the debts, along with back taxes, which until that point, I was not aware that we owed. After we moved back to Springville, we lived in three rental homes while paying off a portion of the business bankruptcy. We had sold our home there to pay off debts. Eventually, years later, we were able to purchase a foreclosure home.

Penelope had moved with us during each move during the sixteen years she lived with us. We began shuttling things from the rental house to our new home. Last to go were our three cats, Penelope, Nigel, Susie, and our pop-up camper. By this time on moving day, it was already dark--and we were all exhausted. Our small Honda had a trailer hitch, and Sean attached the pop-up camper to it--I was designated driver. "Come on, Jasmine. Help me round up the cats. It's late and we need to get everything out of here and into our new house," I said wearily, pushing my hair back and rubbing my eyes. Jasmine and I loaded the cats into the car. We both got in, and away I drove, towing the pop-up camper. Sean and Cassie had gone on ahead in the moving truck to empty the last load. It was yet another move in yet another car for Penelope. She warily sat on my lap with her front paws on the driver door, peering out, wide-eyed and nervous.

Nigel and Susie were perched on the back seat, staring out the back, and Jasmine rode beside me in the front. Slowly I headed down Sherman Street at about twenty-five miles per hour, not quite confident in towing the pop-up trailer at night. Sean hadn't bothered to hook up the brake lights or turn signals; originally, we had hoped to move the camper during daylight hours, but the day got away from us. We just wanted to get everything off the rental property and turn in the keys at the end of this very long day.

As the car and camper advanced slowly down the street, other cars began passing us, which I considered normal, since we were going at such a sluggish speed. Eventually, drivers tooted their horns, some even making hand motions, pointing behind us. I was exhausted from moving, determined to reach where we were going. I stared straight ahead, hoping not to encounter a police car, since our brake lights weren't working. I tried to make it through the intersections on green lights, so I reduced the pace to a crawl, inching up to the intersections.

In the back seat, Nigel and Susie meowed in distress, standing on their hind legs, peering out the windows. Penelope, her face a stern mask, was mute, staring out the driver side window, perched on my lap. She felt it her duty to oversee this latest moving venture.

"Mom, look!" Jasmine exclaimed, turning around to look back. "That's why they're all honking at us!" I glanced in my rear-view mirror. To my horror, the camper was popped out completely on both sides. The canvas bucked the air current, flapping wildly. Here we were, traveling down the street at night with a fully-extended pop-up camper--approximately twelve feet in width--pulled by a small Honda loaded with three cats peering out different windows and two women riding in the front seat.

"Oh my gosh! I don't know what to do, except keep driving slowly and hope we make it!" I exclaimed. I didn't own a cell phone yet, so I couldn't call Sean for help. There was no way I could pull over to a pay phone with a fully-extended camper in tow. As we passed each block, the camper seemed to fill up with even more air, like an expanding balloon. It appeared as if it could just float away, carrying our little car and all of us with it, disappearing into the inky night sky. I slowed the car down even more, to about fifteen miles per hour, and drivers continued to honk and point. I ignored them, staring straight ahead, pretending to be oblivious to it all. Penelope scowled fiercely at all the passing cars, as if to protect us from the onslaught of pointing fingers. Nigel and Susie meowed piteously in the back seat all the while. They knew that something was amiss. Jasmine sat quietly in the passenger seat, nervously glancing backwards every few seconds.

At long last, we reached the new house, and as we pulled up, Sean looked over his shoulder as he carried a chair from the moving truck. "What the heck?" He yelled out, and then doubled over laughing. I'm sure we made a silly sight to behold with our three wild-eyed cats peeking out of a car towing the huge popped up camper. Thankfully, we arrived without further incident.

***

This move was our last as a family with our nanny cat, Penelope. It seemed that Pens realized that we were finished wandering—her human children were safe at last. Only then did she relent, and after a year or so living there, she died peacefully in her sleep at age seventeen. She had endured a rather rough life as a nanny cat, with the additional stress of all the moving and transitions. She always did her best to watch over her charges and was a loyal companion to the end.

Our move did nothing, however, to stem the unrest that Sean felt towards me. I suspected that he was involved with someone else again. Cassie, too, was barely concealing her resentment. In less than a year, she would unveil her plan to leave us.

Thirty-five

2002

"Mom, I want to find my real mom—my biological mom." I was in the laundry room, folding clothes. At those words, I stopped and put down the towel I was folding—and with it, my heart flipped.

"Are you sure you want to get involved in this, Cassie?" I feared her rejection tugging at my conscience.

"Yes. I have to know. Think how different my life would be now if I had been raised by her-- no eye accident. I would have sight in both eyes. I could go into the air force like I always dreamed of doing. Instead, here I am, a young woman with a disability." She looked at me accusingly, her statement cutting to my soul.

"Cassie, I'm so sorry. It was a terrible accident—you understand that, don't you?" My eyes filled with tears that wouldn't stop; I covered my face, waiting for her reply. My plea hung in the air for countless moments. She said nothing.

Coldly, she riveted her gaze at me, her face a mask. "But with my real mom I would have two good eyes." Her voice was flat.

"Oh Cassie! I wish I could change that day for you—I wish you had two good eyes also. What can I do to help you now?" In my mind, I relived that fateful day when Cassie, age two, was in my care, and she fell, the glass from the coffee table breaking and blinding her eye. I had taken Cassie to an eye specialist every year since. No longer did the doctor recommend eye surgery. After a series of them, spaced six months to a year apart until she reached age twelve, there was no success in restoring sight to the scarred tissue of the eye. Cassie didn't seem to mind as a child. She played happily and did well enough in school. Then she entered the teen years. Even then, she seemed to cope well, but read slower than most her age, managing to pass her subjects in school with C's. At age eighteen, shortly after graduation from high school, everything changed. She had grown into a tall, lithe, beautiful young woman, her black hair still cropped short, with dark eyes peering out from thick, mysterious lashes. However, Cassie retreated into a private place all to herself, becoming sullen and withdrawn. She lashed out at the three of us when we attempted to talk to her and had become a moody, sulky version of what once was a vibrant, outgoing girl.

Cassie spoke again, jolting me out of my reverie. "I'm leaving here next week. I've saved enough money from my job at Dairy Queen to pay for a one-way ticket to Bozeman, Montana. That's where my mother lives now. I found her on the internet and she knows I'm coming." Cassie looked through me as if I no longer existed for her.

"But—" I trailed off, not knowing what to say. I was stunned—yet had always feared that this day would come, after seventeen years of loving Cassie with all my being, of believing that she was my child. Now I realized I was deluding myself.

"I have to know," she continued. "I have to find out how different my life would be now if I had been raised by her. No eye accident—how totally better my life would be now without that." Her angry scowl placed the blame on me. "I would have sight in both eyes," she repeated. Her bitter statement cut me; my heart was slashed—I clutched at my chest. I had no words to express my sorrow at the pain she also was enduring. I didn't know what to say--what words were adequate?

Moments passed in silence before I could speak. "Cassie, I'm so sorry--it was a terrible accident. I wish it had never happened, but it did." I realized I had already said that, but said it again, wishing I could think of something to change her mind. Cassie stood there, coldly surveying my emotional pain and tears, detached--sulky. She was a teen in resentment mode. I kept folding clothes—a reflex to attempt to create life as normal. *How could I blame her? Would I feel the same in her situation?* I held these thoughts inside, willing myself to say something wise.

* * *

Somehow, I knew this day would arrive. But how does an adoptive mother, who pours her life into a child, ever come to terms with it beforehand? It was a fear that I hoped and prayed would never happen. "But what if…" I trailed off, not knowing what to say or how to say it. I had dreaded this day for all the years of loving this girl, of thinking she was my daughter and no one else's.

"Nothing you say will change my mind. I'm leaving. I may not ever be back. Don't try to make me come back because it won't work. I'm eighteen now and can do what I want."

Helplessly, I stood and stared at Cassie. I leaned against the washing machine, my tears falling onto the newly washed clothes piled onto the dryer. She turned then and charged out of the laundry room.

* * *

On the day she left, my heart simply broke. Cassie wouldn't even allow Sean or me to take her to the bus station, saying that she would catch a city bus to the interstate bus terminal. She left with only a backpack of essential belongings, instructing me to get rid of the rest of her things. She bade a quick goodbye at the front entry—no departing hugs or kisses—and firmly shut the door behind her. Jasmine, Sean, and I stood in the entryway helplessly, all the oxygen seeming to leave the room. We stared at the closed door, willing it to open again. Maybe Cassie would have a last-minute change of heart. We listened and waited, immobile. None of us spoke; we just fixed our eyes on the wooden door. Could Cassie change her mind and come walking back through the threshold? Sadly, the door remained closed.

I turned my gaze at last, to Sean, who continued staring at the entrance, his jaw set but twitching slightly, no words coming from his mouth. Jasmine ran to her bedroom, slamming her door, and I stood there, wringing my hands until they turned red and hot. Cassie was gone from our lives.

Thirty-six

Cassie

I thought the bus would be full, but I have an empty seat next to me. I like that—not having to talk to anyone or be polite. So, I'm gone from Washington and on my way to Montana. The bus will pass through Idaho first. I've only been there once, and never to Montana, but I looked at pictures of Montana online. Majestic and beautiful--lots of open space. I could hardly wait until the day I turned eighteen. Then Mom and Dad would have no say as to what my plans were. I've been planning this departure ever since I was fourteen, two years after I had my last eye surgery. That's when Dr. Hummel gave up on restoring sight to my bad eye. My real mom would never have let that accident happen to me in the first place. She would have been watching over me constantly, and not relying on a stupid cat. I am anxious to meet her now, after all these years. What is her house like.? I hope to live with her for a while, until I figure out my future.

I'm still disappointed that the air force didn't want me. They were certain that none of the branches of military would take me because of my blind eye. It was pointless, they said. So now what will I do with my life? After I settle in with my real mom, I'm sure it will all work out. Maybe she will have some ideas for me. I do love working on cars. Maybe something like that will be good—at least for a while, but I heard that most shops want a mechanic to have formal training. Not sure where I can get that in Bozeman, but my real mom will know. She'll help me.

Thirty-seven

Tully

> *"I love cats because I enjoy my home; and little by little, they become its visible soul."*
>
> — Jean Cocteau

Susie, my female cat, is my "soul sister." Our hearts are as close as two different species can be as she lies curled next to me, purring. Her paw reaches out to caress my face, her little claws extending despite herself. She knows that they hurt me sometimes, but they are part of her gesture of love and pleasure.

Her main goal is to play and be happy all the time, her little trill asking me to pick up her toy on a wand every time I pass her in the living room. Jet black and double-coated, every hair in place, she has wistful green eyes and a wisp of fur where most cats have a tail, as she is a Manx. Petite, her small paws reach out to me each morning at 6:00 a.m. to awaken me for affection and play.

We're soul sisters--oppressed in many ways by the men of our house. Nigel, our large Manx male of tiger stripes, looks and acts more like a wild bob cat striking out his territory. He allows Susie to visit me in my room only in the mornings. He rarely allows her to trespass into the family room, viciously pouncing on her until she retreats to her designated area in the living room. There, like an exiled princess, she sits in repose with her toy, watching us with sad emerald eyes peering out of velvety ebony.

I, too, sit in exile. Sean reigns in the family room all night, with TV on, sleeping on the sofa. I am not allowed to trespass on his mind or emotional state. If I try, he lashes out with "claws" of anger, and I retreat to my room in the back of the house. His heart and mind left me a long time ago. I don't know where he went or how to get him back. He shut me out of his life as lover and soul mate-- lets me into his thoughts only as roommate. I watch him, as the months slip by, with sad turquoise eyes, and sit like an expelled princess, holding my heart out to him. I wait for his eyes to really look at me and smile; to hold me in his arms, to give me the love and strength that once was there.

Part Three

Thirty-eight

2003

"Cats are connoisseurs of comfort."
— James Herriot, James *Herriot's Cat Stories*

After Cassie left, the house seemed unnaturally silent. No one spoke to one another for a week or so; we just went through the motions, the three of us trapped inside our own thoughts. *How was Cassie? Will she ever call? Doesn't she care about us?* Week after week crawled along in a blur. Jasmine and I eventually talked, especially about her day-to-day events at school. Something impenetrable, however, came between Sean and me—but no words were said. We ate our meals separately, and he spent his nights in the family room, falling asleep with the T.V. on. He kept a blanket there, and the sofa became his bed. I realized, at last, that Cassie had been the major connection between Sean and me—all the years of caring for her, first in adoption, and then through her many eye surgeries. Now she had rejected us to live with her biological mother. Something invisible divided Sean and me. We still had Jasmine, and for that, I was very grateful. She kept the days on a normal routine, and of course, we loved her as much as we did Cassie. Cassie, however, had brought us together as parents in a way that was difficult to describe. She was our first, as well as adopted, and then the one with a major injury.

***

Over time, even sharing Jasmine with Sean wasn't enough to hold our disintegrating marriage together. It had been a year since Cassie had left--still we heard nothing from her. The void in our home and hearts remained unfilled. In the meantime, Jasmine was growing up. In contrast to Cassie's dark features, Jasmine had long, strawberry blonde hair and intense blue eyes. I was baking her a cake for her fifteenth birthday, reflecting on the day Cassie walked out on our lives. Jasmine was thinking about Cassie as well. "Mom, do you think Cassie remembers that today is my birthday? I miss her, especially on my birthday and at Christmas. She needs to help me celebrate."

"I know, Jasmine. We all miss her. I'm sorry she isn't here to be with you on your birthday. I wish she would at least call you." She looked sadly at me, and I saw a tear slip down her cheek. Too bad on her fifteenth birthday. What could I do? I didn't know how to reach Cassie.

The next day, Sean and I argued over why Cassie had left. "You know, you should've been watching her more closely that day; she never would have had the accident with her eye," Sean accused bitterly. So, there it was—the unspoken accusation—held only in his mind until the day Cassie disappeared. From that day on, he had been holding me responsible for her loss of sight in her one eye, and for Cassie leaving us forever. Now, a year later, he also assigned the brokenness of our marriage to me as well. His accusing stares and silences pronounced me guilty.

"I can't bear you blaming me!" I yelled in return. "I love her from every molecule of my being. She is my daughter, for God's sake!"

"But why did you let it happen?" Sean gaped at me, imputing me with his eyes.

"I left her alone for only a few moments. Pens was watching over her for me." I sniffed, my tears taking over again, realizing how foolish my excuse sounded out loud.

Sean snorted. "The CAT? Come on, Tully! A cat couldn't prevent an accident like that. What were you thinking?" He frowned at me derisively, making me feel so small—so idiotic.

"I couldn't watch her every single second of her day and you know that."

"So now she's gone from our lives forever, and hates us for her one-eyed sight. Good job, Tully. Maybe you need to receive the best adoptive mother award of the year." He jumped up, thoroughly disgusted, and grabbed his coat. He gave me one last icy stare and slammed the door behind him. From that day on, we drifted farther apart.

Still, there was no word from Cassie—no phone call, no email, no nothing. I felt as though she had died, and my heart died with her. No longer did I care about Sean. Each day, his cold empty gaze blamed me for Cassie's absence. The three of us ate our meals in silence at first, and then, Sean began to show up so late that Jasmine and I ate our evening meal without him. We were all going through the motions as a family unit, but one important person—Cassie-- was missing. It was all my fault.

***

I saw the text messages on Sean's phone. He was in the shower when his phone rang. I picked it up, but instead of answering it for him, I scrolled through the text messages. There it was. Not Joanne this time, but a Kate. I had already guessed that something was going on, since he always came home late, never acknowledging me, and never came to bed. He acted like a ghost in his own house—even with Jasmine. It was like neither one of us were here—he looked through us, then disappeared for long stretches of time. Seeing the messages for real stabbed at my heart. This Kate was suggesting that they meet at her place tonight. I gasped—the pain was too raw. Again? How many times could we hurt one another? I, too, had my brief affair when he first did, all those years ago, but now? I set the phone down quickly, as if it were hot to the touch. I picked up my dust cloth, pretending to be dusting the family room where Sean had inadvertently left his phone. Usually he carried it with him into the shower. I kept my face down, furiously cleaning away every dust particle in sight as he strolled into the room, smelling of soap and aftershave—the kind I liked.

He glanced over at me suspiciously before snatching the phone and shoving it into his pocket. "I'll be late." Then he stomped out. That was the most he had spoken to me in weeks.

My mind was reeling, my heart, aching. I had to have a plan for all of this. How long could we live under one roof as strangers? Jasmine was in her room, getting ready for school. I needed to ask her what she was willing to do. "Jasmine, could you come here a minute?" Despite my resolve, I was crying. It just hurt so much to see the text message of Sean's new affair.

Jasmine walked in, the surprise on her face evident as she saw my tears. "What is it, Mom?"

"I know you need to get to school, but this is important. I'll drive you to school an hour late, if you can talk with me for a bit."

"Uh, sure, Mom. What is it? What's wrong?" She hugged me, and we sat down on the sofa, the one Sean used for sleeping. I smelled the scent of him on the cushions, making what I had to say even more difficult.

"I know that ever since Cassie left, it has been hard on all of us." I took a deep breath. "Your father seemed to leave us at that point, too."

"I---I know that, Mom. He's rarely here, and when he is, he never talks to you or me, right?"

"Exactly. But if you had to choose between us for where to live, who would you choose?"

At that, Jasmine snapped her head back, shock and horror on her face. She buried her head in her hands, refusing to look at me for a few terrible minutes. When she finally looked up, she said, "Isn't it enough for you that we lost Cassie to our family? Now you're asking me to choose between the only two people left in my life?" She leaped up abruptly, a gazelle bolting to her room for safety, and seized her backpack. "Mom, I can't deal with this now. That's your problem. I need to get to school; the bus will be here in one minute now." As she fled from the house, I heard her retreating footsteps.

I never felt so alone. Finally, I allowed myself to cry. There was no one to hear me except my cats, Nigel and Susie. They ambled over, snuggling on either side of me—always sensing when I needed them most. I had to make the decision alone—I was at the point of losing my own sense of self. I knew that deep inside that I couldn't go through another betrayal from Sean and stay married to him. It was just too hard this time. Our lives were crumbling, and with that, Jasmine was the victim in it all. I petted both cats at the same time, the tears of despair flowing freely. What had we done to ourselves?

Thirty-nine

Jasmine

You'd think I didn't even matter to Mom. All she ever talks about is wondering how Cassie is doing or why Dad is out so late at night. I'm here--always have been. I'm the real daughter—not the adopted one who left to find her biological mom a year ago. Mom looks right through me, like I'm not even in the room, constantly crying over Cassie leaving and how she must be to blame. I do well in school, and I think I'm pretty good at the piano. Mom never compliments me for those achievements, acting like they are expected from me—no big deal. At my piano recitals, Mom just sits there with a ridiculous grin pasted to her face, her mind far away, worrying about what Cassie might me doing or where she might be.

Dad is rarely here but when he is, at least he asks me how I'm doing in school. I'm going to talk to him tonight when he shows up.

***

Around midnight, Dad slipped into the house quietly. I waited up for him in the family room, studying for my physics test. After we talked, I decided to move out with Dad. He said he can drop me off at school and pick me up each day since his new apartment is out of the school district. I like that idea. At least I can talk to him in the car every day. Mom ignores me when we are in the house together, so at least I will have one parent. No more drama or wishing for Cassie to come home. Cassie is a grown woman, for crying out loud—she would be nineteen by now. When I'm that old, I hope to be in college, preparing for a good job, like teaching music. I bet Cassie works at some dead-end job like stocking shelves or changing oil in cars at a mechanic shop. Who knows? I'm just sick to death of Mom not caring about me.

Mom doesn't know that Dad and I are moving out yet. She'll find out tomorrow. It's no wonder Dad found someone else. Mom drives him crazy with her neurotic rants and her obsession with her cats. It gets old. Plus, we both feel that she doesn't really care about us.

Then there is her weird brother, Luke. I never met him—he left before Cassie or I were born. I guess he's my uncle, but who cares? Mom still carries on about him being missing from the family. I wouldn't be surprised if Mom or Grandma drove him away too--both of them are a little extreme.

Forty

2003

"I'll be back Saturday to get the rest of my clothes," Sean said, stomping out of the house, leaving Jasmine sobbing. I halted—immobile and statuesque -- feeling nothing and saying nothing. I looked down to discover that I was gripping my coffee mug so tightly that my knuckles had turned white. What more was there to say? Yesterday had been the day of the argument, and now Sean was exiting our lives.

Jasmine looked at him go longingly, but he had been resolute; he had someone else in his life now. Hoisting his suitcase, he riveted his eyes from me to Jasmine before turning to leave. After he exited, Jasmine turned to me. "Mom, this is all your fault. I hate you for this! With that, she sprinted to her room and flung her door shut. I was paralyzed for a moment—I couldn't make myself move. With all that she and I had been through, from Cassie's disappearance to Sean's extended absences, I thought she understood.

Obviously, I was wrong. Tears blinded my sight as I managed to stumble down the hall and gently knock on Jasmine's bedroom door. "Jasmine honey, may I come in?" I sniffed, willing back the tears.

"No! Go away—forever! I'm moving in with Dad. I can't stand this toxic house anymore!"

I hesitated, taken aback. All along I had assumed that she would opt to stay with me if Sean and I broke up. "Jasmine! You can't mean that. I'm coming in." I gripped the handle, turning it, and stepped inside. Jasmine was already throwing things into her backpack.

Jasmine refused to look at me; she just kept adding clothes to her backpack, and when it was full, grabbed an overnight bag from under her bed, stuffing clothes into that as well. "I'm sorry, Mom. Dad and I already talked about this last night. He found an apartment for the two of us and I'm leaving too. There's just too much drama here." Jasmine didn't look sorry at all; I was shocked.

"Jasmine, I…" My words just stuck in my mouth. How could I convey what I felt? How I loved her more than life itself? How could she do this to me? More to the point, how could Sean carry out this against me? *Think, Tully*. No words would come; I seemed unable to move, and watched the packing process, willing her to stop and hug me. But she didn't.

"Okay. I'm done for now. I'll come back later when Dad does and finish taking my things." Jasmine threw her backpack over her shoulder and grabbed the pink overnight bag I remembered so well. I had bought it for her to take to sleepovers with her friends when she was in middle school. My throat choked; I couldn't speak now if I knew what to say, which I didn't. Coughing, I made my way to the bathroom for a tissue, thinking desperately for what to say.

"Jasmine. I--I love you." My voice cracked, but I continued. "I need you here--what will I do without you?" I felt so abandoned, so alone. Timidly, both Nigel and Susie crept over from their familiar napping places by the living room window. They seemed to sense something of importance was going on. "Nigel, good boy," I said, grateful for the distraction as he brushed against my legs. Susie sat in the hallway at a respectful distance, apprehension on her face.

"Oh, you'll think of something. I just can't stand it here anymore," she said, dismissing me and heading for the front door.

"Please, call me? Let me know where you are?" I pleaded. I knew I sounded pathetic, but couldn't help myself.

"Yeah, I suppose, if Dad says it's okay." With that, the front door closed softly. I stooped down to gather my cats into my arms, crying into their lush fur. I had lost them all; but at least I had Nigel and Susie with me. They were always loyal. The three of us sat on the sofa for a long time; I finally turned on the television and watched sitcom reruns, trying to lose my thoughts. The nagging what ifs kept cropping up. Where had I gone wrong? I switched the T.V. off. The house became eerily quiet—conversations of the past hung in the air like ghosts, haunting my every movement and thought.

I slipped down the hallway, peering into each of the girls' bedrooms. The beds were made, and posters were still on the walls. Cassie's room held all her essence, even after her being gone for a year. Her spartan taste was evident in the sharply tailored grey spread on the bed. She had tacked up classic car pictures on the wall, reflecting her passion for cars, as well as air force recruiting posters. She had been so disappointed that her blind eye had disqualified her from enlisting. In a way, I was relieved about that. She was kept out of certain danger.

I moved on to Jasmine's room—frilly and feminine, a complete contrast to Cassie's, replete in a pink floral and fluffy lace comforter. There was a framed photo of a black grand piano mounted on the wall. Jasmine's dream was to own at the least a baby grand someday. My parents had purchased the old Baldwin upright piano for me years ago, with the hopes of my children learning to play piano. Jasmine had become proficient on it, but always hoped to own a grand piano, the size used in concert halls. As I wandered on into the family room, I noticed the old Baldwin piano standing in the corner. I walked over to it and stroked it reverently, even lifting the cover on the ivories, playing a few lonely chords. Resting on top of the piano were photos of Jasmine at various recitals, smiling into the camera. Next to one picture was the dragonfly figurine Sean had purchased with me on our first date. I picked it up; its iridescent wings glistening and winking, seeming to scoff at me in mockery. Quickly, I set it back in its place on the piano. Then I caught sight of the sofa that Sean used to occupy every night, a blanket and pillow folded up at the end; no one would use them now. I picked up the pillow to put it away, but couldn't help lifting it to my nose. It held the familiar scent of Sean. I took a deep breath, trying to compose myself. I missed him already, even though I didn't want to miss him.

Truly, I was alone--despair hovered at the edge of my mind. I entered the kitchen to make some tea, and the cats followed me. As I waited for the water to boil, I looked over some bills, and the cats meowed softly, as if afraid to ask too much of me. "Sure. Here you go, you two. Have an extra treat of Fancy Feast. I set down their bowls, and poured hot water over my tea bag. Just going through some everyday movement helped. I considered how the bills would be paid; I would have to ask Sean if he still intended to send some of his paycheck to cover expenses here. My paltry check wouldn't be enough. As I sipped the peppermint tea, I decided to call the newspaper and request additional assignments--I had to keep moving or the melancholy would take over and dominate my thoughts.

Before I could dial the number to the paper, the phone rang. "Oh, hi Mom. What's up?" Mom said that she had some rather big news. Luke, my long-lost brother, had called her after no communication with any of us after twenty-four years! He was returning home for a visit. My emotion was profound: it was like a loved one assumed dead, was alive after all. I was stunned and speechless; I imagine I looked like a stiff mannequin in a store window. I couldn't move or talk for what seemed like an infinity. My mouth moved but no words came out. At last, I noticed that I was crying as I noticed joy and sadness dropping onto the receiver.

I heard Mom asking over and over, "Tully, are you okay? Aren't you glad he's coming? Tully? Say something." Somehow, I couldn't answer—the river just kept flowing from my eyes.

Forty-one

2003

He already looked like an old man. His silver hair was pulled back in a ponytail; it was sparse and receding at the top of his head. His weather-beaten, tanned face was creased from years of squinting in the sun. He waited at the entrance, his large frame taking up most of the doorway, and said nothing--but I recognized him in an instant. "Luke! Is that you? Come on in!" I stood back to let him pass, not sure if he expected a hug or a handshake; I offered neither. Suddenly, we were strangers instead of brother and sister--it was awkward. He still hadn't said a word but stepped past me and stood just inside the hallway. He was a good foot taller than I, and his presence seemed to cast a pallor. I noticed that he wore the same type of jeans and black leather jacket as he had before his disappearance. I attempted to act normal—brisk—as if it were not unusual to greet my sibling who had vanished with no explanation for twenty-four years and then reappeared at my door. Mom had telephoned again this morning to let me know that he was heading over. "Uh, come on in and sit down. I have some coffee brewed up in the kitchen. Would you like a cup?"

"Sure—black." He nodded, shuffling in and surveying the living room. He hesitated, choosing where he should sit.

"Here," I gestured to the easy chair. "It's the most comfortable spot." Uneasily, he stepped over to the chair and sat, sprawling his long legs in front of him, but sitting up straight.

"Nice place." He appraised me, as if registering who I was at long last. "Tully, you look different."

I chuckled, heading off to the kitchen for the coffee. "Back at you," I said over my shoulder. "It's been a few years, you know." I regretted the remark as soon as it came out of my mouth. It sounded like a criticism—I had planned to get off to a good start with this long-lost brother of mine. Already I was chastising him for being gone.

"Well, you know. I always meant to call, but then time got away from me, and it seemed too late."

I returned with two steaming cups of coffee, and set them down on the coffee table. I sat down on the sofa and faced him, then took a sip before responding. "Well, it doesn't matter now. You're here, and it's so good to see you." I smiled over my mug, hoping I sounded warm enough to loosen up the conversation a bit. I was sincere, to a point. I had never understood why he left, or why he never communicated his whereabouts all those years. It was a topic at family gatherings, and no one had an answer. It seemed cruel; our parents had suffered so much, not knowing for certain what had become of him. Speculations ran wild, from Luke dying to living in a prison camp in a hostile land. Year after long year, they hoped and waited. Endless questions flooded my mind, but I held my tongue, at least for the time being. He might make a run for it and we'd never see him again. I didn't want that on my conscience. *Where to begin?* "So, how are you?" *Was that a benign question, or too much?* I shifted on the sofa, sitting back, trying not to look too eager. I took another sip off my coffee and tried to look casual.

"I'm okay. And you?" He took a swig of his coffee, and scrutinized me one more time, as if checking to see if I really was his sister. In turn, I studied his hand encircling the coffee mug. It was strong and tanned, his nails neatly trimmed. My eyes followed up to his face, still a very attractive man, but his features were creased with lines from harsh weather and the passing of time.

"Sure, I'm okay, except that I'm living here alone now, but I have Nigel and Susie—my cats," I explained, nodding toward the hallway.

Nigel could be seen peering around the corner, evaluating Luke. Susie was in hiding.

"Oh yeah? Don't you have two girls or something, and a husband? Mom told me that much." He paused, then added, "I didn't realize you liked cats so much. Heh heh. You've changed."

"Not really so much, and I've always loved cats. But to answer your question, yes, I have two girls and a husband." I wondered to myself how far to go into the topic of my family. "Cassie lives in Montana, and my youngest, Jasmine, moved in with her dad. We--we are in the process of divorce."

"Oh--sure. No worry. You don't have to say more. So how old are the girls? Big enough to be on their own?" He was trying to appear interested in me now.

"Well, yes and no. Cassie is nineteen, and Jasmine, fifteen."

"Isn't one of them adopted? Seems like I heard something about that from Randy a while back."

"Yes, that would be Cassie." I looked down into my cup, feeling the remorse and sadness at Cassie's leaving.

Luke picked up on my emotion. "So, what's up with Cassie? Why is she in Montana?"

"A long story—the short of it is that she left at eighteen to find her biological mom. She never communicates with us, so I have no idea how she's doing."

"Oh. Gotta be rough, right?"

I had to bite my tongue at that remark, given how Luke had hurt my parents at his departure of twenty-four years. "Uh, yes, very." My eyes met his over my coffee.

"Yeah, well, things happen." Luke shifted in the chair and looked down the hall at Nigel. "Cute cat. What's his name?"

"Nigel. Plus, I have Susie, but she's shy, and probably hiding under my bed since you came to the door." At the sound of his name,

Nigel sidled over to me and brushed against my leg. He looked over suspiciously at Luke, ready to protect me if necessary. "It's okay, Nigel. This is my brother." I stroked his head reassuringly. The subject had changed. We skirted around Luke's disappearance gamefully, and then it was time for him to go. "So, are you staying with Mom and Dad or what?"

"No, I'm at the Ramada over by the airport for now. They invited me, of course, but I feel more comfortable in the hotel. Plus, I have someone with me, and haven't introduced her yet."

"Her?" I smiled mischievously, just like we were teens again instead of middle-aged.

Sheepishly, Luke explained a little. "Yeah, she's not my wife. Doubt she ever will be. But we enjoy one another's company. Next visit I'll tell you more about myself. Promise. Let's meet for lunch tomorrow over by the Ramada. I'll buy."

"Uh, sure. Okay. Let me know the time and I'll be there. I'll give you my phone number."

"Already have it." Luke smiled a tight grimace and stood up to leave, finally giving me a handshake. When he gave his hand, I reached up to his broad shoulders and stole a quick hug. I couldn't help myself; it just seemed right. "Good to see you, brother. Thanks for coming." I gazed into his eyes, which were brimming with sadness and years beyond his chronological ones. He truly seemed old and tired.

"See you tomorrow, Sis." He lumbered out the door, quietly closing it behind him. I had rehearsed our reunion together for years, dreaming about it, and wondering what we would say if we met. Was he truly here just a moment ago, or was I imagining it again? It was all so surreal--my long-lost brother back at last.

Forty-two

I entered the restaurant near the Ramada at precisely one o'clock, the designated time, but didn't see Luke at first. Then I looked around the corner, finding him in the bar at a small table, already into his first drink. He saw me enter and motioned for me to sit. "Hey, Sis." He gave me a full grin, not the forced grimace of yesterday. The alcohol was having its effect already. When we met at the house, I didn't notice the scar on his left cheek. I wondered momentarily about that, but looked away quickly, hoping he hadn't noticed me staring. "What do you want to drink?" I hesitated too long, thinking maybe to order a cup of coffee, but he told the waiter, "The lady will l have a glass of wine. Red or white?" He looked at me for an answer. While I thought about my answer, he said, "I'll have another Scotch, straight up."

I couldn't help but raise my eyebrows. "Uh, white, I guess. But isn't it too early?" I felt a little strange. This wasn't the Luke I remembered. But then again, we had both changed over those long years.

"Not where I lived for years. It's past five o'clock there for sure." He chuckled, and the waiter left to bring back our drinks. "Plus, I need a little something to loosen my mind while I talk about the past. This always helps," he said, grinning and lifting his glass. So," he began, "tell me about yourself a little more." Luke sat back, his large fingers around the glass, swirling the potent liquid. Today he wore a blue button-down shirt with the sleeves rolled up. It accentuated his wide shoulders and revealed a tattoo of an eagle on his right forearm. He appeared much more relaxed than he was yesterday in my home. I, on the other hand, felt strained and awkward here, seeing Luke in what looked to be more of his usual surroundings. I only rarely sat in a bar—in fact, only rarely ate out. Nevertheless, I decided to plunge into my past, relieved now that the waiter brought me the white wine. The glass gave me something to hold onto while I delved into my life. I explained to him how I met Sean, and how we agreed to always own cats. I told Luke about our adopted daughter, her accident, and how after being advised that we couldn't have children, I became pregnant with Jasmine.

"We went through some rough married years, moved around many times, and," I paused, taking a sip of the wine. "We both had an affair." I looked over at Luke, waiting for his reaction. There was nothing.

Luke toyed with his glass, waiting for me to continue. "Go on," he encouraged gently. I recounted how Sean was involved in a second affair, and how our marriage had finally reached its inevitable end. By the time I concluded, I was crying a little, and we were both nearly finished with our drinks. Still, Luke didn't comment on my revelations, and simply asked, "Shall we order lunch now?"

At least, he spared me from asking any judgmental questions or any gruesome details. For that, I was grateful. "Yes, let's eat." He ordered a steak and fries; I ordered a cobb salad.

While we waited for our food, I wiped at my eyes with a napkin. "So, tell me about you, Luke. You said you would catch me up a bit." I didn't want to push too hard, but all the same, I was curious. How could a person just walk away from his family for all those years and never communicate?

"Well, my life isn't anything to be particularly proud of. You remember that girl I was dating—Rebecca--from my senior year?" I nodded but said nothing. "Okay." He took a deep breath. "She got pregnant and never finished high school, but she wanted to keep the baby. I didn't want Mom or Dad to know at the time, you know. They would give me 'the lecture.' I just told Rebecca that I would send money to her every month to help support the kid. That's when I took off, joined the army, eventually getting deployed. I was assigned into Special Ops and didn't want to worry the folks--we were sent on many secret missions anyway. I spent most of my time overseas in various dangerous places, mostly in the desert." At that, he chuckled a little, supposing it to be a joke.

"So where exactly did you serve?" I was hoping for a location, but Luke ignored my question, continuing with his story as if I hadn't interrupted.

"I made a career out of the military. I retired a couple of years ago, and here I am." He gulped the last of his Scotch and set down the empty glass on the wooden table with a thud. Then he ate a few fries, since our lunch had arrived, and looked at me for my reaction.

I really didn't know what to say. I had many questions about where he served, what he was required to do in Special Ops, and even more about his child. I ventured, "Did Rebecca have a girl or boy?"

Luke paused a moment. "A girl. I sent money to Rebecca until the girl reached eighteen. She went to a university in California—full scholarship. Occasionally, I sent her something so she had spending money. The girl graduated, and works somewhere in Frisco as an attorney."

"The girl. What's her name?" He sounded so impersonal—his own daughter—just referring to her as 'the girl'.

"Tamara." He shifted in his chair, a scowl on his face. It was obvious that he didn't feel comfortable talking about her.

"You know, I'm sure Mom and Dad would love to know that they have another granddaughter—and one who became an attorney." I smiled slightly, trying to act as if this were just a random idea.

"Maybe. We'll see. First, I need to introduce Amy, my girlfriend. That's enough for this visit."

"Okay. Do I get to meet her as well?" I brightened, trying to appear hopeful.

"Uh, sure. But later—not right now." Before we said our goodbyes, I found out that he had retired in the Portland, Oregon area, and had met Amy there. That meant that he lived only about a three-hour drive from Springville. When Luke stood to leave, I noticed how he towered over me, and noticed that he was probably the tallest man in the restaurant. We walked out together after he paid and walked me to my car. I drove home to rejoin Nigel and Susie, feeling a light-heartedness I hadn't experienced since Jasmine had left. My long-lost brother was back! When I entered the house, Nigel and Susie ran to welcome me. I scooped them up in my arms, nuzzling their soft fur with my face.

"Hi, you two. Let's get a snack and then cuddle on the sofa a bit. Maybe watch a little T.V."

Forty-three

2003

*"When I am feeling low all I have to do is
watch my cats and courage returns."*

— Charles Bukowski

It was during the third week when Jasmine called. "Mom, hi. I made the debate team at school—I just wanted you to know." Tears welled up around the edges of my eyes at the sound of her voice; I missed her so much.

I willed the tears back as I said, "It's so good to hear from you, Jasmine. Good for you, Sweetie. I'm proud of you." I waited for her to say more. There was nothing.

"Thanks, Mom. Gotta go. Bye." She hung up. It was brief, but at least, it was a phone call.

I kept waiting for the phone to ring and to hear Sean on the other end of the line. He would say that he was sorry, and we would get back together. I had it all arranged in my mind. We were a couple—married for twenty-three years. We were married always, no matter what, right? I wasn't sure what my response would be when Sean called, and spent many restless nights playing out various scenarios and conversations in my head. Sean had left me for another woman—again. What should I say to him? The betrayal ran deep, stabbing my heart with its sharp edge; I felt severed in two. After a solid week of tossing and turning in my bed at night, I was exhausted.

I had decided, at last, what to say when he called. It was just too much. He obviously wanted to live separately from me, and he had never forgiven me for Cassie's accident. We had been through marriage counseling after the first time he left me. Now, it seemed that we had no other choice except divorce. It had reached its ugly conclusion. I had hoped that he would initiate the divorce. Perhaps he was beginning the legal process already and hadn't notified me yet.

Another week went by and still there was no phone call. I wanted to call him, but resisted the urge. It was up to him this time, but the waiting seemed unbearable--I felt so alone. Both of my daughters were gone, and of course, Sean. I relied on Nigel and Susie for companionship and even conversation, but even I knew it sounded silly. Regardless, talking to the cats helped. At least, the cats offered unconditional companionship and purrs, asking only for food and a little attention.

It was during the third week of waiting for the phone to ring when Jasmine called to let me know that she had made the debate team. During the fourth week, I received an email from Sean. *"Tully, we aren't making a go of it anymore, so I have filed for a divorce. You should get the paperwork in a few days. Sean."*

That was it—our marriage was over. I stared at the email a few minutes, willing it to contain more in the way of feeling or comfort. It was harsh, brief, and cold. The finality of it tightened my stomach; I felt sick—weak—and I shivered involuntarily. A deep sob erupted from my lips as I reread the email several more times, unwilling to accept that after all these years of marriage, it was over. And communicated through an emotionless email. I tried to find some sort of regret in his words, but there was none. No sorrow, no nothing. It was still all my fault, even though it was Sean who had cheated this time. Yet, I was the one who caused the pain, the destruction of our family through Cassie's mishap. I choked back my sobs and closed the computer. What kind of future did I have now? My entire family had deserted me. Once more, Nigel jumped up near the computer, meowing and insisting that I pet him.

"You know how I feel every moment, don't you, Nigel? Susie awaited at my feet, brushing up against my leg for attention as well. They would help me through this. I allowed myself a good cry, and gathered both cats close. Alone and deserted, I remembered to say a prayer, asking God to help me and to allow me to be with my daughters.

Forty-four

October 2003

I was jarred out of sleep— I realized sleepily that it was the phone ringing. *Maybe it's Sean.* I reached over to the bed table and grabbed the receiver. "Hello". My voice cracked; I was groggy, but instantly heard the voice of the newspaper secretary, Rita, asking if I would take an assignment at the nearby mall. I turned her down--I just didn't feel up to it. Nigel and Susie hovered by me on either side as I lay back on the bed while tears stung my eyes once more. As I lay there in self-pity, the phone rang again, startling me. I jumped, and the cats in turn, leaped down from the bed in alarm, running into hiding. It was my co-worker from the paper and long-time friend, Jennifer. "Hey, Tully. Why haven't you been into the office lately?"

"Uh, hi, Jennifer." I hesitated before answering her question. My head was surrounded by a pity fog. I shook my head to clear it. "Um, uh, I haven't felt well lately, I guess." I knew my excuse sounded lame and fake.

"Okay. Are you all right? You sound sick."

"I'm—I'm fine." My voice trailed off a little. Even I could hear it.

"How about meeting me tomorrow for coffee at Starbucks by the office? Are you up for it?"

"Okay, I guess. Name a time."

"Will eleven o'clock work for you?" I said okay before I had time to reconsider.

I had concluded several weeks ago that Sean no longer loved me. In fact, perhaps, he never did. We were so young when we met and then married. We were infatuated with the idea of love and felt a connection through our passion for cats. When I thought about it, I marveled that we didn't take the step of fostering homeless cats along with adopting Cassie.

What went so wrong? I was angry and resentful at Sean and his girlfriend. Why did he have to continue to hurt me? Why didn't he want to talk to me about our problems instead of just divorcing? We had reached the termination of our marriage; I wept once more for the loss. The divorce paperwork that Sean's lawyer prepared had arrived last week. I had stared at it for three days, then, with a sigh of resignation, signed and returned it by mail to his lawyer. It was in black and white—cold and calculated-- no discussion.

The Daily Messenger, where I received freelance work, sent me fewer and fewer assignments; I stayed home alone, hour after hour, mourning our dead marriage and broken family. I tried to pray, but was God even listening anymore? The hurt was too much as I realized with finality that Sean didn't love me and had turned to someone else. What was her name this time? Was it Kate? It didn't matter really. He had outgrown me and no longer desired me, if ever. He never did apparently, or he wouldn't have betrayed me with two different women at two different periods in our lives. I, too, shared in the blame with my own fling as well. I allowed my mind to go back to that time years ago, regretting ever having met the guy. Eric—that was his name. I had to think a moment to remember.

I slept little and ate even less. My weight dropped dramatically; nothing fit in my closet, but I didn't feel like shopping for new clothes. My old clothes hung off me, and as I looked in the mirror, I observed an old woman, even though I was still only forty-three. I had to cinch up my jeans or slacks with an old leather belt to keep them from falling off. As I peered into the mirror, I noticed dark circles under my bloodshot eyes. I touched my dry, lifeless hair; it looked like burnt straw. I felt lethargic and didn't really care.

***

I stood in the walk-in closet trying on all my baggy clothes the next morning, hoping to find something acceptable to wear out in public that wasn't too loose. I finally decided on a simple pull-on pair of grey yoga pants with a knit sweater in pink, decorated in sparkly glitter. At least, I could get by without a belt gathering up a puffy waistline, and the pink top came down over my bottom. I applied makeup for the first time in weeks and tried to style my straw-like hair. I petted the cats goodbye as they sat by the door, watching me leave, worried expressions on their faces. They sensed my mood--I was fragile. "It's fine, kitties. I'm going off to meet an old friend. Take a nap and wait for me." Breathing deeply, I walked out the door and shut it firmly.

When I entered the Starbucks, I held my shoulders back, lifted my head, and attempted to look more confident than I felt. It was my first time out in a public place in two weeks. Jennifer already sat at a small table, waiting for my arrival. "Hey, girlfriend! Over here." She flashed her contagious smile, and I couldn't help but return it. "You look great!"

"Oh yeah? Well, thanks. I tried to find something decent, but nothing fits anymore."

"Well, you know the solution to that. Let's go shopping after coffee today. How about if we eat lunch first? I'm sure we can find you something new and stylin' in your post-divorce size." She looked so enthusiastic, I had to say yes.

We ordered lattes, and as we sipped on them, Jennifer caught me up on the latest at the newspaper office. It was therapeutic to be with Jennifer—more than I had realized. After an hour, we went to our favorite boutique where she helped me pick out a pair of beige slacks, some jeans, and two nicely fitting tops to go with them, one in black and one in green. I felt better already; now I could get out to do work assignments or go wherever I chose and feel adequately dressed. It was a start.

***

Jennifer also invited me to attend church with her the next week. At first, I declined, but then decided to go—just to get out again. What did I have to lose? On the following Sunday, I attended mass with Jennifer. It felt awkward, since I had never gone to a Catholic mass before. At her church, people stood, kneeled, or sat, and seemed to know just when to do each movement. She nodded at me or nudged my elbow to signal when to do something, so it was okay. I made it through the service without feeling too inept. As I sat there, I was struck by the pervading atmosphere of reflection and inner peace. The people left the sanctuary quietly, murmuring in soft tones only after reaching the foyer. They appeared respectful-- serious and silent. No one rushed up with huge pasted-on smiles to welcome me and ask questions. That was a relief—I didn't feel like explaining anything about my personal situation. I felt welcome just by being a part of this well-ordered service—and I wasn't evaluated or judged. I went with Jennifer the next week, and many weeks after, soaking up the stillness and majesty of the mass, praying in solitude and quietness for my broken family and myself. I left each time feeling a serenity and peace I had never experienced before.

After a couple of months of attending mass with Jennifer, I began to pray for forgiveness for myself. It seemed to be the natural thing to do at that point. Gradually, I decided that I could really get into this tranquil, serene faith. I savored the symbolism and inherent beauty of the candle-lit mass, which provided a time for personal reflection. Love and forgiveness were visible reminders as I contemplated the Christ on the cross. I was reminded of how He too, was betrayed and suffered. After a few more weeks, I asked Jennifer, "Is it possible for me to become Catholic?"

"Well, yes, it is," Jennifer said slowly. "Let's ask the person who arranges classes for new people considering joining the church. I think they have weekly sessions." Jennifer introduced me to Anne, who told me more about the class. I still felt so alone, but took comfort in this venture into peace, love, and forgiveness. The weekly classes introduced me to new people, to new ways of looking at life, and to inner peace and happiness. I attended the classes for a few months, and for the first time in years, I felt good about myself. I looked forward to the day when I could become a member of the church. I realized that I had a long way to go to forgive not only myself but Sean. I kept praying about that and attending weekly mass.

Over time, my anger and resentment subsided. I was ready to meet with Sean and talk things out in a peaceful way, and hoped to ask him to forgive me, as I was attempting to do for him. I realized that I would always love him, no matter how he had hurt and betrayed me. I had wronged him as well. Both of us had made mistakes and wounded one another. Would he feel the same about me, or had he gone a different path since our divorce? I knew he still had his girlfriend, Kate. Maybe it was all too soon for him but I had to try. I would contact him through Jasmine, I decided one Sunday at mass, gathering up my purse and coat to leave. I felt relief and confidence as I smiled at others and walked into the foyer. I was finally ready to move forward with my life.

Forty-five

October 2003

"Tully? It's June." I knew something was wrong—June had never called since the divorce.

"What is it, June? Is everything all right?" Her voice sounded terrible. I braced for bad news but waited for her to tell me.

"Uh, it's Sean—he had a heart attack." June broke down at that point, and I couldn't understand much of anything that she said.

"June—June—slowdown--is Sean all right?" My stomach turned over, hearing her on the other end of the line. She couldn't say more—just held onto the receiver and wept. "June! Tell me what happened!" I shouted at her, trying to get her to calm down enough to tell me. A panic rose inside me; I tasted a metallic bile in my mouth. "What is it?" I demanded. My whole body was shaking with dread.

I finally got it out of her that Sean's massive heart attack had struck without warning while he was out golfing with his buddies. Paramedics tried to save him, but he died on the way to the hospital. The hospital called Jasmine, who lived with Sean, but since she was a minor, the hospital personnel asked for June's phone number to notify next of kin. Momentarily, I resented that—why wasn't I the one called? Then I remembered—Sean and I were divorced. *Oh, right.* A bit ashamed for what I was thinking, I held onto the phone, my breath sucked away in a vacuum of guilt. My lungs needed air--I felt faint from the lack of it. As the news slowly sank in, I asked myself how this could this be. Today was Tuesday, two days after my decision at church to talk to Sean and ask for his forgiveness—and to tell him I would always love him. I was going to tell him--it was a personal promise I had made. *This can't be!* I had it all planned in my mind, rehearsing what I was going to say and how to say it—and I was going to do it this week. I hadn't slept much since Sunday, imagining the conversation Sean and I were going to have. I was hoping to ask Jasmine for his new cell phone number. Now it was too late--my mind reeled with the harsh reality--Sean was gone. *But no! He couldn't be!* Not now. We would be friends—I had it all worked out—we would see one another at holidays and celebrate together with our family. I pictured all of us smiling, sitting around the table together at Thanksgiving and Christmas. I knew of other divorced couples who did that.

It was too much—it just couldn't be possible. "No, no! This can't be true!" I shouted. I heard uncontrollable wailing—eventually realizing that the horrible sound was emanating from me. There was only silence on the other end of the phone--June had hung up.

I stood in the kitchen staring at the phone in my hand. *Why, God? Why did I make a promise that you knew all along that I couldn't keep? Why? Why?* A rage took hold of me at that moment— I looked around the kitchen, the fury erupting without warning. I shouted and screamed, throwing my coffee up at the wall. The mug splintered, and with it, a crater was hollowed out of the wall. I slammed down the receiver, not caring if it broke or not-- I was a woman on a rampage. "Nooo!" I yelled, grabbing my dirty breakfast plate, throwing it as well. It ricocheted and shattered, piercing yet another hole.in the sheetrock.

Nigel and Susie crept in to see the commotion, hunkered down in combat position. Then they both ran off into hiding—Nigel behind the sofa, and Susie, down the hall. My breath came in ragged jags. It was hard to slow down the fury once it had begun. I swept my right arm across the counter; the toaster, coffee brewer, and utensil jar clattered to the floor. I was angry at our broken lives and alienated family, at the years wasted together, of little or no communication, at our tangled lives and affairs with other partners, at God, but most of all, myself. Finally, I finished the howling, but the tears were streaming down my face, and my nose was a slobbery mess. I grabbed several tissues and sat down on a chair, spent at last, and put my head in my hands, weeping softly. Regret and despair washed over my consciousness.

***

The funeral, at least, got us all together at long last. Jasmine had stayed in contact with Cassie so was able to tell her the bad news. Cassie returned from Montana for the service, her first time back since leaving for Montana. Cassie roomed with Jasmine at Sean's apartment while she was in town. Luke attended the service as well, and brought his girlfriend, Amy. It was our first chance to meet her, but in a totally different venue than we would have wished. My parents and Sean's mother were there, of course, as well as Sean's coworkers and golf buddies. We, the family, sat in our own section, a long line up of us, mostly in black attire. Only Cassie dared to show up in a short-skirted red dress-- as always, standing out. Sean's girlfriend, Kate, attended, I heard later, but sat in the back unnoticed. It was a good thing that I didn't know that she was there—I may have given her a piece of my mind.

June, Sean's mother, was dressed totally in black, from her dress, hat, heels and gloves, and sat with us in the family section. She was seated next to Jasmine, her back ramrod straight, her countenance an immobile mask—impenetrable and terrible, partially concealed under a black veil. The lines on her face revealed years of hard work as a single mother and a woman propelled into widowhood at a young age. The grief for her son was deep—fathomless. Afterward, in the foyer, she walked up to me, composed but sorrowful. "Pray that you never lose a child," she said, weeping quietly beneath her veil. "Sean was my only one—now I have no one." Slowly she turned and left, striding purposefully out the door and out of our lives. I stared after her, speechless and red-eyed, my heart breaking at the lone image of her, the slim older woman whom I had never gotten to know very well. I pictured my future, mirrored in June, my own girls continuing to reject me. I would live alone in my old age as well. I wept anew, grieving for June's staggering loss, my fatherless children, and myself, for losing my former husband of twenty-three years--the man I loved. Now, I would never be able to tell him. Sorrow over what might have been washed over me, standing there at the entrance to the church. It was Jasmine who finally took me by the hand, and led me out, my eyes blinded by tears.

∗∗∗

All the family except June met for a late lunch after the service. It was subdued, broken only by an occasional attempt at conversation or light chuckling at some recalled memory. Everything seemed contrived—forced--and my mind went into a fog. But at least we were all together for the first time in many years--everyone except Sean.

Forty-six

October 2003

My head was in a fog—no coffee yet. I rubbed my eyes and looked over at the clock on the night stand which read seven-thirty. "Mom, Kate wants to talk to you." It was Jasmine on the line. She was still living at Sean's apartment with Cassie, and I hadn't seen either of them for the three days following the funeral. They seemed to be avoiding me. I didn't know how long Cassie would be in town, but so far, she kept Jasmine company at the apartment. I moped around alone in my house, with Nigel and Susie as my sole comforters.

I knew that Sean had a pension, willed into my name, as well as other financial investments and life insurance that he had kept in my name as beneficiary. I knew that from our divorce decree from his attorney. I would survive alone financially, at least. However, that wasn't my concern now; I just wanted my daughters back.

I realized suddenly that Jasmine was saying something about another person wanting to talk to me and I forced myself out of my reverie. "Who? What in the world are you talking about?"

"You know-- Kate." Jasmine paused, hesitant and embarrassed to say more.

"Kate." I stopped, trying to focus. "Oh, Kate. That woman. I have nothing to say to her. Tell her that." Now Jasmine had my attention-- I felt the bile rising in my throat again. My heart raced even without the coffee.

"Mom, just let her talk to you. She wants to meet you at the Denny's over by Juniper Boulevard. Just do it, Mom. She really wants to share something with you."

"Why? Is my pain not enough as it is? Does she want to add more to my wounds? I thought you still cared a little bit for me, Jasmine. Do you have no empathy at all? She took your Dad away from me forever." My mouth let out an audible cry, and the tears welled up once more. I had managed to keep them away when I didn't think too hard about the situation. I tried to sleep as much as possible, hold my purring cats on my lap, and watch sit com reruns on the T.V. It had worked until this morning.

"Mom, it will be fine. Trust me. She's a nice person, really."

"Hold on. Let me put the coffee on. I can't think straight." I struggled into my red, fuzzy bathrobe and stumbled into the kitchen. The cats followed, meowing, sensing that it was breakfast time. My days were not as synchronized at they once were; I used to feed them promptly each day upon awakening at six.

Jasmine seemed to be more patient with me than usual, waiting on the other line for me to get the coffee going. Soon, the gurgling began, and I pulled off half a cup while the brewer finished the rest. "Okay. I'm ready." I took a sip, wondering what Jasmine had to say.

"Mom, Kate really needs to talk to you. It will be good for both of you. She suggested ten o'clock either today or tomorrow. Go." Jasmine had never sounded so assertive before—I was taken aback. I paused but continued to grasp the phone in my right hand, the coffee mug in my left, the mug suspended in midair. I sat down at the table, placed the coffee on it, and tried to gather my thoughts. I covered my face in my hands. *What do I say? I don't want to see this woman.*

"Jasmine, why? I really don't get it."

"Just trust me, Mom. You'll get it when you meet with her. It won't hurt you, I promise."

"All right. I'll get it over with today. Tell her. Today at ten, Denny's. By the way, how are you and Cassie doing over there by yourselves? I realize she is nearly a grown woman, but I miss you both. Come over."

"Uh, yeah. We might do that. I'll ask Cassie. Bye, Mom." She hung up, and I sat for a moment, staring at my phone. Then I realized I had to prepare to meet "the other woman" and dashed back to the bedroom closet, going through my clothes, searching for the perfect outfit. I settled on a pair of black slacks with cream sweater, but only after trying on three other outfits first, and tossing them onto the unmade bed. After putting away the clothes that I had decided against, I made my bed and tidied up the house a little. I showered and carefully applied makeup, and dressed in the slacks and sweater, preening in front of the mirror. I wanted to appear the well-dressed woman, even though Sean had discarded me for her. As I looked at my reflection, I felt that I could never measure up. There were a few streaks of gray in my auburn hair and tell-tale lines appeared at the edges of my eyes. However, I was doing this under duress at Jasmine's insistence. *Whatever I look like will have to do, I guess.*

Denny's wasn't that far away, so I waited until 9:40. I didn't want to get there too early. I left the house with a pat on each cat's head and drove to the restaurant. As I entered, I observed a woman in a booth alone. I wasn't sure what Kate looked like, but the woman was watching for someone, and smiled as I glanced her way. She looked somewhat younger than I—maybe five years—and had shoulder length, wavy brown hair. She was pretty, with wide brown eyes and full lips. My heart sank—I had imagined that she would be beautiful--and I was right. The budding self-confidence I had mustered up for the occasion evaporated, but it was too late to turn around and go home.

Kate spoke first. "You must be Tully. Hi—I'm Kate." She stuck out her hand for a shake, and I didn't know what else to do but take it.

"Uh, hello. Yes, I'm Tully."

"What a quaint name—Tully. Is that a nickname or your given name?" She smiled gently—I studied her face to see if she was making fun of my name but didn't see any condescension.

"Actually, it's short for Tulia, but I always prefer Tully." I sat down across from her in the booth stiffly, not waiting for her to invite me. I clutched my purse to my chest as if it were a shield, too nervous to sit without something in my hands. I stared across at the woman who took my Sean away forever. She even had long lashes and a perfect oval face. She kept beaming kindly at me, and stirred her tea. Soon the server appeared, and I ordered tea as well. Tea seemed more soothing than additional coffee. I sat silently, wondering what we were going to talk about next. I hoped I could maintain my composure, and not get weepy about Sean and the funeral--she would probably want to talk about that. I was weary of thinking about it.

"So, I suppose you are wondering why I asked you to meet with me." Kate's face fell, her mind at a loss for words. "I, uh, wanted to share something with you." She toyed with her napkin, looking down, and seconds elapsed. I waited, stirring lemon and honey into my tea. The sound of the spoon tinkling in the cup was strangely reassuring. I took a sip. She looked up and took a deep breath. "Well, here it is. Sean would come over and yes, we spent time together and slept together, but I felt like you were there the whole time. You see, he always brought you up in our conversation; in fact, you dominated all our talks. He could never resist mentioning you." Kate paused, shuffling in her seat uncomfortably. "He-- he loved you so very much, and never got over the fact that you two couldn't make a go of it." Kate stopped, and looked at me for reaction. I kept my face a blank. I needed more information before I could react to this.

"Okay. Go on—I'm listening."

"So, he told me he loved you and wanted to make things right with you. He wanted to ask your forgiveness. You see, I felt so inadequate, so inferior to you. You were his wife; the one he truly loved. I was only a diversion. He told me he wanted to break up with me, and ask you for forgiveness, and tell you he only ever loved you." She sighed softly before continuing. "That was right before his heart attack. He never had the chance." Kate reached for a tissue in her purse and dabbed at her eyes. I sat there, as if in a stupor, all emotions a blank. *What was she saying? Did Sean want to tell me the same thing I had hoped to say to him? How could that be?*

It hit me with the force of smacking into an invisible glass door. "So, you're telling me that he said he wanted to ask my forgiveness and tell me he loved me, right before his heart attack?" I still couldn't believe it, especially coming from "the other woman."

"Yes," she said simply, again looking down at her twisted napkin. "I-I hope you will forgive me as well," she finished.

At that, I nearly snickered, but managed not to, noticing her obvious distress. I could be mean, but not that mean. I wanted to say something, but didn't know what just yet-- it was too much to take in all at once. "Yes, well, our lives as a family were ruined." Suddenly I felt unbending; self-righteous. Here was "the other woman" asking me for forgiveness. I had no family life now, no husband, and my girls wanted nothing to do with me. I was reduced to a middle-aged woman living alone with my cats.

"I realize that you have lost it all. Sean felt so badly about it. He felt responsible for it, and was planning to tell you. He—he told me that he had blamed you for Cassie's partial blindness, and that's why she left home at eighteen to find her biological mom. He realized that was wrong of him. That's why I requested our meeting," she finished softly. Kate sat straight, staring down into her tea, her eyes reddened with penned up tears. "I—I was just hoping you might forgive me as well. But it's a lot to have to forgive between what he did--and what I did." She looked small, vulnerable, seeming to shrink into the booth, still twisting the frayed napkin. Her luminous eyes held sadness and regret. I gazed into her eyes, which mirrored much of my own pain.

"I—guess--I guess-- I'm not the only one holding onto pain and regret. I—I think I see that now. What was in the past is the past. Maybe we all need to move on. Do you agree?" I wasn't sure how much I could sincerely forgive at this point; I felt stony and immobile, dead to feelings. Somehow, I realized that I had to try to forgive even without the emotion. Still, I said nothing yet.

"So, I wanted you to know all of this. Sean loved you, not me. Do you think you can forgive him or me?" Her large brown eyes gazed into my own.

"I already forgave Sean. I had planned to tell him that, but he died before I had the chance."

Kate exhaled sharply. "What about me?" she pleaded, twisting the napkin until it broke into shredded pieces. How could I refuse?

"Yes—yes. I—I forgive--you," I managed to say, not knowing how sincere it was, but at least saying it to this tortured woman. Kate reached across and attempted to grasp both of my hands in hers. I wasn't quite ready for that yet and refused to take her hands into mine. Quickly, she withdrew her extended hands and placed them in her lap.

"Thank you, Tully. I hope we can get past this, and even be friends." She grinned bravely, hoping I would agree with her. She placed her right hand across the table, hoping I would take it this time. I did reluctantly—her hand was soft but cold. I held on just a moment before letting go.

"Perhaps. Let's just see how it goes. I hope that we can be friends of sorts, but more than that, I hope I can get my daughters back."

"Me too. Thank you, Tully. Sean was right. You are an incredibly strong woman. It's no wonder he loved you so much."

Kate and I said our goodbyes, exchanging phone numbers before leaving. It was the least I could do, even though I doubted I would call her any time soon. The biggest test loomed ahead—regaining the love and respect of my daughters.

Forty-seven

October 2003

"Cats have it all—admiration, an endless sleep, and company only when they want it."
— Rod McKuen (poet, *Stanyon Street & Other Sorrows*)

The pungent smell of bacon sizzling roused up Nigel and Susie. They sauntered into the kitchen, heads moving side to side, noses sniffing, softly meowing. The table was set with floral placemats resting underneath three white plates, a pitcher of freshly squeezed orange juice positioned in the middle. Cassie and Jasmine were arriving for breakfast, or brunch for me, at 10:30. My heart sang at the prospect of the three of us together over a meal, and I hummed a tune for the first time in a long time. The girls were coming over! I stirred up a batch of scrambled eggs and sliced fresh cantaloupe, placing wedges on a platter. English muffins rounded out the meal, but I waited to toast them until after the girls arrived. I brewed a pot of coffee, and sipped on a mug of it, nervous that they might not show up—it was ten thirty already.

At ten thirty-five, the doorbell rang. I sprang to the door and swung it open—perhaps a little too eagerly. There they stood: Cassie, unsmiling as usual, and Jasmine, a fixed grin on her face. "Hi Mom, we're here," Jasmine said flatly, stepping into the house first. It had been more than a year since Cassie had walked out this door and out of our lives at age eighteen, never setting foot here until now. Silently, she followed Jasmine into the house.

"Come in, come in. Breakfast is ready. Are you hungry? I just need to toast the muffins and then we can eat." My words all tumbled out in a nervous jumble. *Get hold of yourself. Don't be so happy.* I felt giddy—silly really. My girls were here together at long last. "Want some coffee while you wait?" Cassie mumbled a reply, and Jasmine declined by shaking her head. I poured a cup for Cassie and handed it to her. She kept her gaze down, refusing eye contact with her good eye, but held out her hand to accept the cup. "Sit down. I'll have your plates ready here in a jiffy." To smooth over the moment, I felt I had to keep up the banter. No one spoke but me. "So, what have you two been up to on your own at the apartment? Staying out of trouble?" I chuckled, trying to get a response at levity.

It wasn't working. Cassie shuffled in her chair, saying nothing at all, and Jasmine just replied, "Oh, Mom."

"Well, you're here and you don't have to hussle up something to eat. It's ready now." I began serving up the portions, and placed them in front of each girl. Then I served up a plate for myself. "Let's say grace, shall we?" No one answered, but I said a short word of thanks, and then we began eating. The scraping of forks on plates was the only sound.

I started to think I would never get them to enter into a conversation until Nigel walked in, sidling right up to Cassie. He meowed softly, purred, and rubbed against her leg. Susie watched him from the safe distance of the refrigerator. Cassie stroked Nigel on the head. "He remembers me after all this time." As she spoke softly, a tear slipped down her face. "I can't believe it. He really knows who I am." Eventually, Nigel walked up to Jasmine as well, greeting her with the same purr and leg rub.

"Of course he remembers you. Both cats have missed you. They go into your room and lie on your bed—Jasmine's bed too," I smiled gently. Nigel returned to Cassie, and lay down at her feet while we continued our breakfast. Here I had been so nervous about our get together, and it was Nigel who initiated our conversation. Gratefully, I looked Nigel's way, and reached out to pat his head. Cassie noticed Susie as well, who looked on shyly from the kitchen, and got up to pet her and bring her over to the table.

"Both cats look and act the very same," Cassie said, smiling slowly for the first time. Jasmine nodded in agreement. I noticed that she looked relieved to see Cassie loosening up and talking. I, too, felt relieved as well. Before long, we chatted about Jasmine's school, my work, and eventually, I asked about Cassie's life in Montana. It took a little prodding, but she finally shared about her job at a Ford dealership in Bozeman. I could tell that she liked her work and found out that she had completed the training to become certified in the Ford brand as an auto mechanic. I noticed that her hands were rough, strong, and callused as she grabbed onto her fork. Her fingernails were clipped short, which I assumed, was for easy cleaning of mechanic grease.

Before the girls left, they walked down the hallway and peeked into their old bedrooms. For the most part, each room was decorated just as they had been when the girls occupied them. Cassie's room still had the classic car posters on the wall, and Jasmine's, the framed grand piano picture. The beds were covered in their old spreads, the somber, tailored grey on Cassie's, and the fluffy pink floral of Jasmine's. I heard them exclaiming pleasure at what they saw as I cleared the breakfast dishes from the table. I smiled to myself, silently humming the song that was still in my head. They took their time examining things in each room, while Nigel and Susie followed them from room to room. Their voices sounded so normal in the house once more, filling my home with life. I didn't want the morning to end.

All too soon, the girls departed, saying that Cassie had to call her boss to request additional time off. She was expected back to work in two days but hoped to get a few more days here in Springville.

After they left, I rested on the sofa and hugged Nigel to my chest. His purring was calming; soon Susie joined us to recline beside me. I was so thankful for the two little furry creatures, who somehow did their part in bringing me a bit closer to my daughters. Maybe things would take a turn for the better. Thanksgiving was just a few weeks away, and the thought of the whole family coming together gave me hope. I smiled at the idea, and petted Nigel and Susie fondly. In their feline way, they had helped reunite us. I set about making plans to hold the holiday meal here and invite all the family.

Forty-Eight

November 2003

Jasmine moved back in with me after Cassie left for Montana, of course, since she was still a minor at sixteen, and Sean was gone. As we chatted together over dinner her first day back, I ventured the question I had been afraid to ask. "Do you think Cassie would come back here for Thanksgiving this year?" I was hopeful but didn't want my dream to be dashed. I looked up from my plate nervously and waited for her answer.

"Umm, I don't know. Why don't you ask her?" *Typical teenage response,* I decided. Jasmine continued eating the grilled chicken, picking at her peas, and not saying anything more.

"Well, did she leave you a phone number, so I could call her?"

"I have her number, yes. I'll ask her if it's okay for you to call her." She looked back at me, at bit defiant.

"All right, you do that. Let me know." *For heaven's sake. My own daughter, and I have to get permission to call her?* But I let it go. These were tricky times and I had to go slow. At least, Cassie had agreed to eat breakfast in my home last week.

"It's just-- it's just that Cassie made me promise not to give out her number. You know, a sister thing," she finally admitted.

"It's okay. I get it. Just let me know."

***

As it turned out, Jasmine just made the call for me and invited Cassie to a Thanksgiving get together at my house. Jasmine said she was coming. Excitedly, I began to plan, as well as invite the rest of the family. It felt strange to be able to call Luke and invite him after all those years. "Sure, Sis. I'll be there if I can bring Amy. Don't want her to be alone for the Thanksgiving holiday. You know me—family man at heart."

I chuckled at his sarcasm. "Of course!" I said, happy for as many people to share in the day as possible. For too long, our family had been a fragmented and rather sad, small group.

"I'll bring the booze, if that's okay."

"Uh, sure!" I hadn't thought of alcohol. Leave it to Luke, but oh well, fine. At least he was coming! How exciting after so many years. The girls didn't even know this uncle of theirs. They saw him at the funeral and that was it. Next, I invited Mom and Dad, who were happy to have someplace to go for a change. We had celebrated Thanksgiving at their house each year for as long as I could remember. I called Aunt Ruby in Idaho, hoping that she might even come. After she picked up, I said, "Hey, Aunt Ruby, this is Tully. Say, I'm having Thanksgiving this year at my house. Can you come?"

"Of course, Tully. Anything for my favorite niece. I'll just book a flight in first class and enjoy myself all the way with champagne."

"Great! Thanks, Aunt Ruby. Let's be in touch."

At last, I mustered up the courage to call Sean's mother, June, who always had excuses for never joining in on family get togethers. I still pictured her, the solitary, hunched over figure dressed in black, leaving the funeral. When I called her on the phone, her voice rasped out a hello. "June? This is Tully."

"Yes," her voice croaked.

"Say, I'm having Thanksgiving this year, and I'm hoping you will join us. We really want all the family to attend. So far, my girls are coming, Luke, and my folks. Also, Aunt Ruby." I paused, waiting for her to say something. Nothing. "Will you join us? The girls would love to see you, I know—and I would too."

There was breathing on the other end as she considered. "Uh, I don't know. I'll have to think about it. I might be working that day; I don't know yet."

"Oh, June. Please come. Ask for the day off. We really miss seeing you. It will be a chance to renew and reconnect. As you know, Cassie has been away for so long, and now she has agreed to be here. Please." There was silence. Then I added, perhaps a little too brightly, "And Luke too. He's been away for twenty-four years and now lives in the Portland area, so he can also attend family events. He's bringing his girlfriend, Amy. We can all meet her as well."

"Why would I care about meeting his girlfriend? What's it to me?" June was even more anti-social than ever. However, when Sean was alive, she sometimes tried to act like part of the family. Sean confessed to me once that his mother had a drinking problem. Perhaps she had gotten worse since his death. I realized that her life had been torn apart by losing her only child.

"Well, think about it." I urged gently. "I'll check with you again in a few days, okay?"

"Do what you want. Gotta go. Bye." The phone clicked off. Undaunted, I said a simple prayer that June would come to our Thanksgiving meal and reconnect with everyone—especially Cassie and Jasmine. If I could just get everyone in one place at one time—my place—it would be a Thanksgiving to remember.

"It will all be good, right Nigel and Susie?" The three of us snuggled on the sofa, and I dared to dream of a family reunited—our family.

Forty-Nine

Cassie
November 2003

My seat for the plane ride back to Montana is three rows from the back. I'm sitting next to an elderly woman, and I hope she doesn't want to talk. I need to process my thoughts after Jasmine and I left the breakfast at Mom's. After leaving her house, I drove back to Dad's old apartment with Jasmine where we were rooming together. Our ride back was silent, as I reflected on how Nigel and Susie had never forgotten me—still considered me as part of the family. I tried so hard to put my adopted family behind me, filing them away as part of my past. Even Jasmine isn't my real or blood sister—only a concocted, artificial one. My goal was to find my real mom, my real roots. I told myself that was all that mattered to me—that the discovery would make me a whole person.

Seeing how Nigel and Susie came up to me so easily reminded me of Penelope, my childhood "nanny cat." She was always there for me—even when my accident happened. She did her best to help me, I'm certain of that.

I blamed Mom for the accident and loss of sight in my left eye, and so did Dad. What a spiteful screwup of things. What did Mom really have to do with it? Regardless, I escaped to Montana and attempted to make a go of it. Finding Stephanie, my biological mom, wasn't too hard. The big shocker is that she looks nothing like me—she's white. I guess my dark complexion is from my real dad, whoever he is. Maybe someday I will look for him, too, to understand more about who I really am. But Stephanie is a mess and a huge disappointment. When I arrived at her house, a shabby trailer in a run-down mobile home park, she just looked at me with a blank stare, left the door open, and returned to her soap opera and her bottle of whiskey. Her eyes were glazed, as she mumbled incoherently. I walked through the open door, not knowing what else to do at that point. She didn't seem to register who I was, and didn't care. She has never cared about me in all the time I have spent there in Bozeman. I am just someone interfering in her life. When she isn't sleeping off a drunken binge, she has some creepy guy staying over. Sporadically, she works at an all-night truck stop as a waitress, collecting enough tips and wages to call in sick and get drunk again. When I showed up at her door, I became a burden for her, but I had nowhere else to go at first. The jerks she brought home from the truck stop sickened me. Each time, she would claim that the guy was "the one." I couldn't stand living there. I found a low paying job at a fast-food place, earning enough to move out into a rented room. I had no money for a phone, so I was completely out of contact with everyone back home. I worked hard, got a scholarship at a community college in their mechanic program, and completed the training as a certified Ford mechanic. From there, getting a good job with Ford was easy. I have good wages, good benefits, good hours and weekends off. With all of that, Stephanie still didn't care about me at all—she ignored my existence.

Springville. What a joke it was for me to run off and out of the lives of those who really cared about me. My mom there had taken care of me since I was only one or so, and loved me as her own--so did Dad. It didn't take long, living in Bozeman, for me to realize that Mom, Dad, and Jasmine were my real family— not this drunken floozie. But how could I explain that to them and come crawling back? Then Jasmine tracked me down by calling Stephanie. Dad had died.

I assumed that the family would always be there, waiting for me when I decided to return home. I never thought about Dad dying, or anyone, for that matter. I didn't know how I would feel about Dad dying until it happened. He was always there for me growing up. We had a connection; he understood my love of cars, and we worked on my first car together in the garage sometimes. The car never ran, but it was cool to work on it. I missed him so much in Montana. I just thought he would always be there for me when I came home.

Going home to Springville showed me something—especially when I saw Nigel and Susie. I know it sounds silly, since they're only cats, but something clicked on in my brain. The cats remembered me after all that time. Cats do their best but they're not perfect. Penelope did her utmost to watch over me and so did Mom. I see that now. I guess accidents just happen. I need to get past my resentment—and love Mom while I can. With Dad passing away, I realize that now—but it's too late for him. So, maybe I'll move back. Why not? I can ask for a transfer and start fresh with people who really love me. Jasmine is a good kid, too. I've missed her. We've lost out on telling stuff to one another like sisters do. I guess I love her too. Grandma and Grandpa, Grandma June, all of them. I want to be around them again. I even enjoyed getting to know Uncle Luke. Things are what they are, and I'm surviving on one good eye.

Just then the stewardess came around to Cassie's seat on the plane. "Would you like something to drink?"

"Uh, yes, please. I'll have a coke." Cassie made up her mind in that moment. She was flying to Montana to arrange to move back to Springville, to her family. Stephanie didn't want her—she never did.

Fifty

Thanksgiving 2003

"Grandma June, will you come over to our house again soon?" Jasmine asked. The meal was over, and we had all moved into the family room. Luke lit a fire in the fireplace where Nigel had already found his favorite spot. June sat on a straight chair, appearing a little tense. Jasmine approached her and took her hand, looking down at her fondly. Cassie nodded at Jasmine's question in agreement, sitting in a chair near June.

"Well, maybe," June said. "Depends on when I work."

This Thanksgiving was a beginning of many firsts in our lives. June was carrying on a conversation with Cassie and Jasmine, seeming to derive pleasure from them as her granddaughters. I saw her smile--also a first. Luke chatted with Dad, and even Mom. He loosened up a little after his second drink of Scotch and shared the drink with those who wished, among them, June, who took a long swig before setting her glass down. Aunt Ruby smiled and nodded when Luke offered her a little Scotch. She lifted her glass to him good naturedly and took a sip. He brought a couple of bottles of Chardonnay as well, which I served in my best wine glasses. Everyone seemed jovial, so I didn't mind that serving wine at our Thanksgiving meal was also a first. My parents had never allowed alcohol of any kind in their home. I dared to glance their way, but they didn't seem to care, only asking that their glasses be filled with water instead of wine and beamed good naturedly at Luke. They were just thrilled to have him around for a holiday. Amy seemed the quiet type, smiling and nodding when someone was speaking. She was pretty and petite, with long, black hair and lustrous eyelashes. She appeared to be about ten years younger than Luke, which would make her around thirty-seven or so. Her face lit up whenever Luke turned to face her, or touched her arm in an intimate gesture. It was plain to see that she adored him. Amy brought her six- year- old son, Thomas, which was a surprise to us. No one had mentioned a child, but here he was. Thomas hung onto Amy, refusing to move, until I motioned for him to pet Nigel. He barely touched Nigel, but grinned up at me, caressing Nigel's soft fur. "Soft'" was all he said.

"Grandma June, what do you say?" Jasmine asked again.

"Well, like I said, maybe."

"I'll take that for a yes. Maybe we could go to the mall or something, or have lunch. Could we do that?" Jasmine's eyes shined with anticipation.

Cassie suddenly chimed in, "Good idea! Let's go before Christmas."

June looked over her glasses at Cassie. "Well, I thought you lived in Montana, Cassie. How will you go with us?" Her low, raspy voice caught everyone's attention. All of us, including my parents and myself, overheard her and stopped the simultaneous conversations. The question hung in the air—how would Cassie go to the mall on a whim with June and Jasmine?

Cassie looked around the room, a little embarrassed that we were all waiting on her answer. Luke set his drink down, watching and waiting. He stared over at Cassie with an amused expression. "Well, um, I have decided to move back to Springville. I put in for a transfer to the Ford dealership here in Springville. It was approved, and I'll be moving here in two weeks." She looked down, and then got up to go over to Nigel and sat on the floor with him and stroked his side.

Luke cleared his throat. "Uh, great Cassie! Glad you finished your wanderings earlier than I did." He grinned, then raised his glass and took another sip off his Scotch.

I couldn't help myself. I ran to Cassie, stooped down where she was seated by Nigel, and grabbed her in a fierce hug. "Cassie. Welcome back home!"

"I'm not here for sure yet," she chuckled, breaking free of my embrace. Everyone in the room laughed good naturedly. Cassie was coming home!

***

Christmas arrived on the heels of Thanksgiving, spirited and hopeful. Traditionally, we met at my folks'. This year we agreed to hold Christmas at my house, due to Luke's insistence on bringing in his beverages. It just wouldn't feel right to impose those on my parents. So, I invited everyone back. Even June said she would be there. The mall shopping day turned out to be a success, and June and the girls shopped for hours, buying gifts for the family as well as clothes and makeup for themselves. It was a first to have their Grandma June to shop with them. Many times, over the years, they had gone with my mom, Vicki. Mom was good about giving the shopping trip over to June this time. Mom wished to gather the whole family for Christmas, and June was part of the family. Having Luke return to us was her dream come true. Add to that, Cassie was back.

We sat around the family room on Christmas, opening gifts. There was a crazy tangle of wrapping paper, ribbon, and empty boxes. It was too tempting for the cats, and soon, they were jumping into the sparkly, noisy rattle of paper and boxes, and then sprinting down the hall with bits of ribbon dangling from their mouths. While the cats dashed madly around, we continued to open gifts. There was one last small gift, resting inconspicuously on a tree branch. Luke motioned for Thomas to retrieve it and give it to Amy. "What's this?" Amy asked, clearly taken aback as she stared at the golden wrapped box. As she opened it, Luke fixed his gaze on her, awaiting her reaction. It was a sparkling solitaire-diamond engagement ring. Amy gasped. "Will you marry me, Amy?" Luke asked simply.

"Yes—yes!" We all laughed and clapped. Thomas looked at us all, a bit bewildered. He ran back to the safety of his mother's side.

It dawned on us all at once: there would be a wedding in the family! Mom took Thomas by the hand and gave him a peck on the cheek. I saw the realization in her face--a grandson at last. Promise of more family and more love to go around.

At the end of the gift opening frenzy, June said, "Jasmine, I haven't heard you play the piano. Play something for us, will you?" A hush fell on the group, as we all gave Jasmine an inquiring look. She had never played for us at a family gathering.

"Okay, but only because *you* asked, Grandma June." Jasmine smiled shyly, and opened a songbook, turning to Christmas songs. "I'll play a few Christmas carols, but I don't know them well. You all have to sing with me." With that, Jasmine began with "The First Noel." We all joined in, a somewhat discordant motley of carolers, but we smiled, and sang out heartily. Truly, it was a "first noel," with all of us together. Nestled among the Christmas greenery on top of the piano, was the dragonfly figurine, a reminder of Sean and our first love. June's smile at Jasmine and Cassie touched my heart, but when I glanced at Mom, she had tears in her eyes, radiant, as she stared at Luke, her long-lost son, home at last.

Fifty-one

Vicki
December 2003

I'm afraid. I'm afraid of losing Luke again and his soon-to-be step-son. So, I'll try to stay in the shadows for now and let them plan the wedding. I'll show up but that's all. I can't stand the thought of Luke walking out on us again. It would be too unbearable. My heart will just break in two and never recover.

I'm afraid Luke sees Ray and me as judgmental parents, and that may be the reason he left the first time. I'll never understand for sure I suppose. I must just step aside and watch from a distance.

God knows that I would love to hug Luke, Thomas, and Amy-- and never let go. I want to treat Thomas as my grandson and spoil him a little--but need to hold back. Maybe someday. Just knowing that we can be with them during special holidays is enough for now.

In all the twenty-four years that Luke had disappeared from our lives, never did I imagine that he would return, get married, and have a step-son. I'm so happy! My son is back, plus I will have a step-grandson! I prayed for Luke to contact us every day during those long years. I had nearly given up when out of nowhere he called us. Twenty-four years…such a long time. I was afraid of what to say or think. Why did he walk out on our lives? All I know is that he's back, will be married, and we will have a grandson to call ours. I love my two granddaughters, Cassie and Jasmine, but this makes our life even more complete.

Winter

The sky spits snow, miniscule icy granules.

Frost clings to rooftops and grass, white as the hair on an old woman.

Trees stand, naked and swarthy, a stark reminder of old age and death to follow.

Winds rattle the trees' arms- shivering from the blasts—but they are spared no mercy.

Relentless, the gales continue, as humans also bend in submission, holding onto hats.

At long last, spring rains deliver the land from freezing temperatures

A welcome balm, coaxing the trees to bud once more.

Epilogue

November 2017

"A dragonfly to remind me even though we are apart, your spirit is always with me, forever in my heart."

— Author Unknown

The problem was that the old Baldwin piano, the family heirloom, refused to go into Jasmine's new house—an unanticipated irony since she and her family were moving to a much larger home. "It won't fit through the hallway," John proclaimed after unloading the piano into the new garage. John looked nervously from me to Jasmine, sensing that we expected him to somehow squeeze the upright piano into the house.

"You're kidding, right?" I asked, mentally surveying the size of the doorway and hall. Then I studied the piano, noting its width and depth.

"No, I'm not kidding. It won't make the sharp turn. It has to stay here in the garage." John and his two friends who were helping nodded in agreement. John sighed, looking exhausted and defeated. He and his buddies had just moved the family's entire possessions—furniture, innumerable boxes—their total worldly possessions. I could tell from my mental calculation of the doorway, hall, and piano that they were right—there was no way. Jasmine had yearned for a bigger house for her family of five for years after living in a small, modest home in a declining neighborhood. After several years of dreaming of a bigger home with a large yard, she and her husband, John, purchased a four-bedroom house on a large lot. The property overlooked a green meadow where Jasmine could watch a sunrise every morning. It was perfect. There were more rooms in the house than they had furniture for.

"How about if I call a professional piano mover? Surely, they will have the right equipment and know how to get it into this big house," I said, desperately trying to think of a way to get the piano inside the house. "The piano will be ruined in no time out here, especially with winter coming."

John looked puzzled, not understanding what I meant. "Pianos have to be preserved in room temperature and low moisture, John," Jasmine explained.

"I'll pay for the movers if they can do it," I reassured them. "We need to try to keep Baldwin in good shape or he won't be good for anything except to be thrown away. I love this old piano." Jasmine looked over at me sadly. She loved it too. The next day I began calling piano movers. Surely there was one willing and able to get a piano into a large house, even if it meant bringing it in through the narrow front stairs or back deck. As I talked to various movers, they asked for pictures of all possible entry ways, hallways, the piano, and measurements of each. It kept me busy gathering all the necessary data and correspondence. Meanwhile, the days grew colder, and the Baldwin piano stood patiently in the garage, abandoned, accumulating tools and dust on its top which once held family photos and the glass dragonfly figurine. I fretted as each day brought colder weather conditions outside as the piano sat in the unheated garage.

I hired a piano tuner, Bill, to drop by to assess the old Baldwin, ascertaining that the possible moving expenses were warranted. Bill assured me that the elderly instrument was indeed in good functional condition, needing only a routine tuning. The disappointing thing was that after checking back with three moving companies the answer was the same. The piano wouldn't fit into the house, unless we risked collapsing the back deck from the sheer weight of the upright. Jasmine and I agreed it was too great a gamble, given possible injury as well as rebuilding the deck.

Reluctantly, I relayed my findings to Bill, the piano guy. "We can't get the piano inside my daughter's house. I downsized a few years ago, moving to a smaller home. I had already purchased a small spinet piano for my new and smaller house, so I don't have room to take it back. Do you happen to know of someone who is looking for one?"

Bill paused a moment before saying, "Well, as a matter of fact, I do know of a family who needs a piano. The children take piano lessons from me and need one to practice on. I'll pass along your phone number if it's okay with you."

"Of course," I agreed, certain that they wouldn't call right away. To my surprise, however, a woman named Vera called within minutes, asking about the piano. She explained that all but one of their six children were adopted, and they couldn't afford to spend much on a piano. "Are you able to pay a little something?" I asked, knowing, after Bill's assessment, that it was, after all, a fine old upright.

"Well, yes, we can," Vera answered.

"Let me call my daughter to see how much she wants for it. I'll get back to you soon."

When I talked to Jasmine and explained about the family who needed a piano, I asked her how much she wanted for it. "Since they must pay a piano mover, just let them have it," she answered."

"You're sure?"

"Yes. It's expensive to move," Jasmine said.

Vera was ecstatic when I called her back. "Oh, thank you, thank you! We have been praying for a piano and you and your daughter have answered our prayer! We will call the piano "Baldwin" too. It will look beautiful in our English Tudor home with our dark mahogany woodwork." Vera went on to say that they lived in the older, stately neighborhood of homes toward the heart of the city, very close to where I first received the piano from the family friend who had also lived in that neighborhood. Our Baldwin was going back to the same area, after thirty-five years and many moves. It would be the Baldwin's home going. When she told me that, I was humbled and grateful that our piano would go to such a nice place.

I still felt anxious that, in early December, the temperatures were going down day by day. Baldwin needed to get into the warmth and dryness of a home. At last, the moving day was arranged. I met the movers at Jasmine's house--she was at work and asked if I could be there to see it go; she would be too sad. I watched as the men carefully loaded Baldwin. My eyes began tearing up despite my resolve to see the piano loaded successfully. Watching them push the instrument up the ramp of the truck, I recalled all those moves over the years with this kind, old friend. Sean had carefully lugged it around to all our new homes with no incident—no injury to the piano or to anyone helping him. I stood there, witnessing Baldwin's final transfer out of my life. I regretted that my grandchildren never learned to play the piano. That had been my dream and Jasmine's as well. As the sturdy piano disappeared into the truck, I whispered, "Goodbye, Baldwin." After all the joy the piano had given to us, I felt I had let it down. Baldwin was the one and only thing I had of any value as an heirloom to pass along. Now, he was leaving us forever.

Tears were wet on my cheeks as I thanked the movers and lowered the garage door. I kept asking myself why the piano wouldn't fit into this large house—perhaps we hadn't explored all possibilities. I couldn't dwell on the question for long, however, since I had promised to call Vera when the truck was headed to her house. "Vera, Baldwin is on his way," I said to her on the phone between sniffles. "And I'm crying. Sorry."

Soon, she called me back when Baldwin had been unloaded into her house. "Oh, Tully! Baldwin is here! Can you hear him? We're all crying now as we see and hear the piano. It's beautiful!" I heard the unmistakable sound of the piano in the background, and tears fell once more, but this time, the drops were a mixture of sadness and joy as well. Baldwin's melodious and resonant sound would live on in a good home, and not land in a trash heap. I had learned that many pianos of that vintage ended up there.

"Yes, I hear Baldwin. I'm crying too."

"This is such an answer to prayer," she went on, as both of us, who had never met in person, wept together over the old piano. "We promise to love Baldwin as you do," she proclaimed. "Now my son can practice before he plays for the church services." A few weeks later, Vera, Jasmine, and I met for lunch to get acquainted. She shared photos of her family and Baldwin together. We also made plans for Jasmine and me to visit Baldwin in his new home.

On the following day of the piano transport, a cold snap settled into the region. Roads were too icy for travel, and temperatures dropped dramatically. However, it was comforting to know that Baldwin was out of the cold garage, safe and warm in his new home, just in time for Christmas. I observed the soft snowflakes falling soundlessly outside my window, thinking about the Baldwin. I imagined the melodies of age-old carols welling up once more from the old piano, with all the loved ones in Vera's large family gathered around. I was happy to consider that I had gained a new friend in Vera.

As I sat on the sofa, watching the snow fall, my present cats, Sebastian and Mandy, lounged on either side of me, purring in contentment. Sebastian was a large, tabby Manx, and Mandy, a small calico, also Manx. Though their names and colors had changed with the passing of time, I still took comfort in my felines and hoped to, always.

I glanced up to the mantel over the warm fire to see the little glass dragonfly in its place of honor there instead of on the Baldwin. The figurine seemed to wink at me, reflecting the fire and soft light of the nearby lamp. The dragonfly reminded me of the promise of good times-- the happy ones, with Sean and my girls. It was a promise that I would keep, even though Sean was gone.

It occurred to me that to give away something loved is also a way of receiving. Giving away the Baldwin demonstrated a small Christmas miracle of giving and receiving. All of us had gained something and were blessed. Our family would once more gather together at my house for Christmas—my brother, Luke, and his family, Cassie, Jasmine, her family, and all the rest.

Snowflakes continued to float down from the heavens, a wondrous reminder of the reason for the Season.

A Thank You for Quotations Borrowed

www.brainyquote.com (cat quotes)

www.cattime.com (50 famous quotes about cats)

www.cattipper.com (cat quotes)

www.pinterest.com (dragonfly quotes)

www.whatismyspiritanimal.com

(dragonfly quotes and sayings)

Acknowledgments

I would like to thank Marlene Loisdotter for her invaluable expertise, encouragement, and editing advice. Her ongoing inspiration is a motivating force in our writing group.

Appreciation goes to everyone in our weekly writing group for their pithy comments and helpful ideas as I worked on this writing endeavor. A big thank you goes to friends and family for their positive support and faith in me as a writer. For all of you, I am grateful.

CPSIA information can be obtained
at www.ICGtesting.com
Printed in the USA
BVHW081516020519
547071BV00003B/298/P